SIMS

Book Two:
The Portero Method

F. Paul Wilson

Book Two:
The Portero Method

F. Paul Wilson

SiMS

Book Two:
The Portero Method

F. Paul Wilson

CEMETERY DANCE PUBLICATIONS

Baltimore

❖ 2001 ❖

Signed Hardcover Edition   ISBN 1-58767-023-2

Manufactured in the United States of America.

FIRST EDITION

Cemetery Dance Publications
P.O. Box 943
Abingdon, Maryland 21009
E-mail: cdancepub@aol.com

www.cemeterydance.com

To Coates Bateman:
Editor-at-large

1

New York City

"Well, it's been two weeks since the inspection," Romy said, "and we're still in court trying to get SimGen to open its basic research facilities. So, net gain thus far from all this effort is zip. Or maybe I should say *zero*—if you'll pardon the expression."

"Any time," Zero said.

They had assumed their usual positions in the dank basement under the abandoned storefront on Worth Street: Zero backlit behind the rickety table, swathed in a turtleneck, knit watch cap, dark glasses, and a scarf wrapped around his lower face; Romy sat across from him. She'd taken extra precautions today to assure she hadn't been followed.

Romy was in a foul mood and she knew it; she'd spent the morning snapping at everyone in the office. And with good reason. The organization was getting nowhere with SimGen. Lots of movement but no forward progress. Like jogging on a treadmill.

And she resented Zero too with his corny disguise and his secrets and his damned elliptical manner. She could sense him smiling at her behind the layers of cloth hiding his face. She wanted to kick over his crummy folding table, unravel that scarf from around his head, rip off his dark glasses, and say, *Let's just cut this melodramatic bullshit and talk face-to-face.*

Usually she didn't like herself when she fell into this state, but today she relished it. She wanted someone to push her button so she could tap dance on his head.

"But 'zero' isn't quite accurate," he said. "Your inspections confirmed that SimGen is treating its sims as humanely as advertised."

Romy nodded. That had been the plus side. Though the young sims led a barracks-style life, their environment was clean and they were well-nourished.

"Humanely," she said. "After spending all that time with so many of them, the word has garnered new meaning in respect to sims."

"How so?"

"Well, so many typical chimp behaviors are missing. The mothers don't carry their young on their back like chimps, but on their hips like humans. And I didn't see a single sim grooming another. Chimps are always grooming each other. I'd think if SimGen wanted to keep the public thinking of sims as animals they would have allowed *some* chimp behavior to carry over."

"First off," Zero said, "it could be learned behavior. If they've never seen or experienced grooming, they might not do it. Plus, sims don't have anywhere near the amount of hair as chimps, so it's not necessary. And if it's genetically linked behavior, SimGen might have engineered it out of them because it would interfere with their work efficiency."

"That sounds typical. Too bad, because it seems to give chimps comfort." Romy shook her head. "No grooming, no sex, no joy, no aggression, no love, no hate . . . it's like they're half alive—*less* than half. It's unconscionable. Chimps laugh, they cry, they exhibit loyalty and treachery, they can be loving and murderous, they can be born ambitious, they can fight wars, they can commit infanticide. A mix of the good and the bad, the best and the worst, just like humans. But sims . . . sims have been stripped of the extremes, pared down to a bland mean to make them workforce fodder."

She closed her eyes a moment to hold back a hot surge of rage. No use getting herself worked up now.

"How do sims feel about it?" Zero asked. "Ever wonder?"

"All the time. I signed to a lot of the young ones during the inspection tours, asking them just that: *How do you feel?* and *Are you happy?*"

"How did they answer?"

"They answered 'Okay' to the first, but they didn't seem to know what 'happy' meant."

"Tough concept. Ask yourself the same question: Are you happy, Romy?"

She didn't have to think about that, not for an instant. "No. No way. My life is one mass of dissatisfaction. And that shouldn't be. Look what the genome revolution has done for us. We'll all live longer because so many genetic diseases have already been wiped out, and days

9

are numbered for the rest of them. Heart disease, diabetes, high blood pressure—if they ran in your family you pretty much had to resign yourself to dealing with them at some point in your life. Not these days. Cystic fibrosis, sickle cell anemia, MS—hell, *nobody* has those anymore."

"Jerry Lewis finally stopped those telethons."

"There you go—something else to be thankful for. And how about cancer—I've personally benefited there. Three years ago I took a screening blood test and learned that although I was negative for breast cancer, I was carrying the gene for ovarian cancer. I underwent therapy and had it spliced out of me. So why aren't I overjoyed with our brave new world?"

Zero said nothing.

The perfect response, Romy thought. If I don't know, he sure as hell doesn't.

She sighed. "Anyway, our inspections were satisfactory—as far as they got. But they could be performing vivisection in that basic research building for all we know."

She'd had two ongoing problems to contend with during the inspection tour. Lack of access to basic research had been the major issue. The other had been the relentless come-ons from Luca Portero; the man had somehow developed the notion that he was irresistible to women, and that Romy's repeated refusals of his invitations to lunch, dinner, and even breakfast were simply her way of playing hard to get.

She didn't mention that to Zero. What was the point? OPRR was through with SimGen for the time being and she probably wouldn't see Luca Portero again for a long time, if ever.

Just thinking about that man now only added to her edginess.

Zero said, "We'll let the courts deal with the basic research issue for now. The good news is that after many man-hours of effort by a number of people, we've finally hit pay dirt on that license plate number you so wisely recorded—a number we wouldn't know had you not thrown them a curve by showing up early that day. A lucky day for us when you joined the organization."

She could feel his praise mellowing her—a little. Always nice to be appreciated, but how sincere was he? Had he sensed her mood and was simply trying to placate her? So damn hard to read him without a glimpse of his face or his eyes. Almost as bad as email. Worse—even email had those annoying little smilies.

"About time something paid off," she said.

"Not a big payday, I'm afraid, but who knows where it will lead. The truck was leased from a firm in Gooding, Idaho, by a private individual named Harold Golden."

"Really." She drew out the word. "What's a private individual from Idaho doing on SimGen's campus?"

"It gets better: Harold Golden's MasterCard is sound, so the leasing company never checked him out; Harold Golden is a good card holder who always pays his monthly bill, so the card company never checked him out. But we did, and guess what? Harold Golden doesn't exist. He's just a name on a credit card account."

"How can you be sure?"

"Can't be one-hundred percent sure unless we find something like his Social Security number belonging to a soldier who died in the Gulf War. That's not the case here. The provenance of his Social Security number

11

appears sound, but can you imagine a man who's doing some sort of business with SimGen who has never taken out a loan of any kind? Who has one credit card on which he charges only one thing: the lease of three trucks?"

"Unlikely . . . but that doesn't mean he doesn't exist."

"I can tell you that he doesn't live at the Boise address he gave the leasing company. And that his MasterCard bill goes to an entirely different address: a mail drop in Hicksville."

"Long Island?" Romy felt a tingle along the nape of her neck.

"At the risk of sounding like an infommercial: But wait—there's more. The investigator I sent to Idaho turned up something else: Harold Golden began leasing these trucks four years ago. The man who runs the company remembers him because he wanted the exact same trucks that had been returned that very day from another lessee. Guess who that lessee was?"

Romy shrugged. "Mercer Sinclair?"

"Close. Manassas Ventures."

"Doesn't mean a thing to me."

"Manassas Ventures was the source of the start-up capital that allowed the brothers Sinclair to get SimGen rolling. Consequently it controls a huge block of SimGen stock."

"And the connection to Harold Golden?"

"At this point, nothing beyond the trucks. But guess where Manassas Ventures has its office."

"Hicksville?"

"Exactly. But it has a strange way of doing business. The company rents space in a small out-of-the-way office building but doesn't seem to have any employees.

Manassas Ventures is on the door, but it's a door that remains locked all day, every day, week after week. Makes you wonder, doesn't it."

"A man who doesn't exist and a business that doesn't do any business. Am I detecting a pattern here?"

"I think so. Ironically, we've been aware of Manassas Ventures all along but never paid any attention. I'd assumed it was simply another of the countless venture capital groups that have popped up since the early nineties—one that happened to get lucky and strike it very rich. But I should have known never to assume anything where SimGen is concerned."

"If Manassas owns a lot of company stock, then it's logical for it to be involved in SimGen doings."

"But logic seems to be taking a breather here. For instance, if you were an investment group with SimGen on your list and flush with capital, what would you be doing?"

"I'd be crowing. I'd have impressive offices to attract new ventures to underwrite."

"Exactly. Yet Manassas Ventures' only address is a deserted space in a nowhere building."

"Almost as if they're hiding."

"They are. Behind Harold Golden. I believe Manassas invented him as a layer of insulation between itself and the truck rentals. And it almost worked. We were just lucky that our investigator asked the right questions on a day when someone at the leasing company was in a talkative mood. Otherwise, we'd never know the Manassas connection."

"But why insulate itself?"

The tingle in Romy's neck moved across her shoulders and down her spine. She sensed the situation moving beyond simply wrong . . . something sinister at work here.

Zero said, "Because I'm betting that Manassas Ventures has ongoing involvement with SimGen's day-to-day workings that it doesn't want anyone to know about. And the most likely reason for keeping an activity secret is that it's illegal."

"But SimGen is one of the richest corporations in the world, with a lock on a unique product"—she hated when sims were referred to as "product," but this time it fit—"in high demand. They're practically *minting* money. They've got it all. Why risk being connected to something illegal? It doesn't make sense."

"It does if whoever is behind Manassas Ventures is pulling strings inside SimGen. Pulling strings that lead to the basic research facility, perhaps?"

That struck a nerve . . . might explain the company's adamant refusal to let OPRR near the building, even with a court order.

Zero went on. Romy could sense him fairly vibrating with anticipation. "And if something illegal or even quasi-legal is going on we may have found the lever to crack open SimGen's wall of secrecy. All because you showed up earlier than expected."

"And caught a worm."

"Maybe a snake. I'd say Manassas Ventures is long overdue for an in-depth probe of its workings and personnel, wouldn't you."

"Anything I can do?"

"In regard to Manassas, no. But as for our friend, Patrick Sullivan—"

"Oh? So he's 'our friend' now, is he?"

Romy sensed a smile behind Zero's muffling layers. "Not a close friend, not a bosom buddy, but . . ." His voice trailed off.

"But what?"

"I don't know . . . there's something about him. Maybe I'm feeling a little sorry for him because he's going through the worst time of his life."

"Really?"

"His girlfriend dumped him, his house is a charred ruin, he's been living in a motel room for weeks, and SimGen is putting the screws to him through his clients."

"How so?"

"Through their general counsel, Able Voss, they're calling in favors, twisting arms, using threats if necessary, all to pressure Sullivan's clients to drop him."

She shook her head in amazement. "How do you *know* all this?"

"I have my sources."

Sullivan's predicament did sound pretty awful, but the shyster deserved it. "Well, don't expect me to shed tears for any lawyer, especially one of the headline-hunting variety who's been taking those sims for a ride."

"Your assessment of him might be accurate, but I've got to hand it to him: He's lost a number of big clients and he's still hanging tough."

"No kidding?" Romy was surprised. "I'd have thought he'd have folded like an old suitcase by now."

"Well, I don't expect him to hold up forever, so I believe it's time we stepped in. And speaking of suitcases . . ." Zero lifted a large metal attaché case onto the table. "I'm hoping the contents of this will bolster his fortitude."

He slid it toward Romy who released the catches and lifted the top. She repressed a gasp at the sight of the stacks of currency.

"How much is in here?"

"Two hundred and fifty thousand."

"What's wrong with a check?"

"I feel a man like Mr. Sullivan—I am not blind to his failings—will require more concrete proof of the seriousness of our interest."

Here was concrete, all right—a whole sidewalk. "How do I approach him?"

"Directly, I would think. I'll leave the details up to you."

Zero rose. A sign the meeting was over.

"But where do I say the money's from?"

"Again, I leave that to your inventive mind. But since I know how lying bothers you, I'm going to make things easier. I'm giving the money to you, no strings attached."

"You're *what?*"

"That's right. To do with as you wish. Buy a house or a fleet of sports cars if you want. It's all yours."

As the shock wore off, she began to understand. "I see what you're up to."

Zero said, "But should you decide to approach Mr. Sullivan with it, I suggest being nice to him. You might find yourself spending a good deal of time with Mr. Patrick Sullivan."

"I can hardly wait." She snapped the lid shut on the money. "That's it? You're letting me walk out of here with a quarter of a million in cash?"

"*Your* quarter of a million. Remember?"

She smiled. This was turning out to be not such a bad day after all.

2

Westchester County, NY

"Mr. Kraft wants to see you in his office," Maggie said as Patrick passed her desk. The strained look on his secretary's face told him the managing senior partner wasn't requesting a social visit.

Patrick's stomach roiled. Great. He was living out of a suitcase, Pamela wouldn't return his calls, his clients were either bailing out with no explanation or giving him ultimatums: dump the sims or we dump you. And now Alan Kraft was waiting for him. Just what he needed.

Well, at least things couldn't get much worse. Or could they?

Patrick laid his briefcase on his desk and glanced around. His office was small, as was his window with its limited view of downtown White Plains. But that left extra wall space for his law books. He liked his office. Cozy. He wondered how long he'd be rating a window if his clients kept heading for the hills.

He walked down the hall to Alan's office, took a deep breath, then stepped inside. A bigger office than Patrick's. Much bigger. Thicker carpet, bigger desk. Lots of window glass, and still plenty of space for books.

"Hi, Alan."

"Patrick," Kraft replied.

No "good-morning" or even a "hello." Just his name, spoken in a flat tone from the man seated behind the mahogany desk. And no handshake. Kraft was something of a compulsive hand shaker, but apparently not today. His blue eyes were ice today, glinting within a cave of wrinkles.

Patrick's gut tightened. This did not look good.

He dropped into a chair, trying to look relaxed. "Maggie said you wanted to see me."

"A serious matter has come up," Kraft said, bridging his hands. "One that needs to be addressed immediately. We all know about the recent exodus of your clients—"

"Just a temporary thing, Alan. I—"

Kraft held up his hand. When the senior managing partner held up his hand, you stopped talking and listened.

"We've been aware of the losses you've been suffering and we've sympathized. We were confident you'd recover. But now things have taken an ugly turn. It was bad enough when it was just your client base that was eroding, but now the dissatisfaction is spreading to the partners' clients."

"Oh, hell," Patrick said. He could barely hear his own voice.

"Oh, hell doesn't even begin to say it, Patrick. Two of the firm's oldest and biggest clients called yesterday to say that they're having second thoughts about staying

with us. They said they'd always thought of Payes &
Hecht as a firm that represented people, a firm above such
stunts—their word, not mine, Patrick—as representing
animals. Who do we prefer as clients, they want to know:
people or animals? Because it's time to choose."

"The sons of bitches," Patrick muttered.

"They may well be, but they're sons of bitches who
pay a major part of the freight around here."

And account for a lot of the senior partners' billable
hours, Patrick thought.

The partners had sat back and watched with clucks
of the tongue and sympathetic shakes of the head as his
client base headed south. No need for immediate
concern: the firm adjusted salaries and bonuses according
to each member's billing, so Patrick's bottom line would
take the hit, not theirs. But when they saw their own
paychecks threatened . . . ah, now that was a different
story.

Not that Patrick blamed them. He'd do exactly the
same.

"I don't think I have to tell you what needs to be
done," Kraft said.

Patrick knew. Shit, yes, he knew.

"And if I don't?"

Alan Kraft merely stared at him.

So that was what it came down to: stick with the sims
or stay with the firm. Mutually exclusive options.

The choice should have been a no-brainer except for
the inconvenient fact that he'd become attached to the
Beacon Ridge sims. He enjoyed visiting them, liked the
feelings that rolled off them—probably the nearest thing
to worship he'd ever experience. But on his next visit

he'd have to tell them he was dropping their case. He'd make up something good, and they'd believe him, and they wouldn't hold it against him, because Mist Sulliman the best, Mist Sulliman never lie to sim, Mist Sulliman never let sim down.

Yeah, right.

Mist Sulliman feel like slime mold.

He fought the urge to grab Kraft by his worsted lapels and shout, *Fuck you, fuck the firm, and fuck all its candy-assed clients!*

Instead, he sighed and nodded. "All right."

He'd lost his house, his girlfriend, and a shitload of clients. He couldn't afford to lose his job too.

"Good man," Kraft said. He rose and thrust out his hand. "I'll tell the others."

Now the handshake. Patrick made it as perfunctory as possible and beat it the hell out of there. Or maybe crawled was more like it. Or slithered. He felt like he'd just ratted out a friend to the police. If the carpet had been shag he would have needed a machete to reach the door.

As he passed Maggie again she cocked her head toward the waiting room farther down the hall.

"New client. No appointment. Wants to know if you can squeeze her in."

"A *new* client? No kidding? What's my morning look like?"

"Empty."

Figured. "Then by all means, 'squeeze her in.' "

A few minutes later Maggie showed a statuesque brunette into his office and introduced her as Romy Cadman. Short hair, dark eyes, full lips, and long legs.

Dressed on the casual side in a sweater and flared slacks under a long leather coat, all black.

Patrick's spirits lifted. Nothing like a new client, and a beautiful one to boot.

Maggie placed the woman's card on his desk: *Romy Cadman — Consultant.*

"I won't take up much of your time, Mr. Sullivan," she said as he rose to shake her hand.

He couldn't find much warmth in those deep brown eyes—at least not for him. All business. A woman with a mission. A *consultant* with a mission.

"Take as much as you need," he said, thinking, I've got aaaaall day. He gestured to a seat. "Please."

"That won't be necessary." Because she remained standing, so did Patrick. "I understand, Mr. Sullivan, that you've come under a lot of pressure from SimGen lately."

"SimGen?" What was she talking about? "No . . . I haven't heard a thing from SimGen."

"Indirectly, you have. They've been contacting all your clients and either cajoling or coercing them into dropping you."

Patrick decided he'd sit now. It sounded so paranoid at first, but only for a second or two, and then it made terrible sense.

"How do you know? How *can* you know?"

"Not important," Ms. Cadman said. "What matters is whether they're succeeding."

"What do you mean?"

She cocked her hip and released an exasperated sigh. "They want you to drop the sims. Are you going to stand up to SimGen, or cave in?"

Cave in . . . hell of a way to put it. At least he knew where Ms. Romy Cadman's sympathies lay. So no way was he going to tell her he'd decided to do just that: cave in.

"May I inquire as to your interest in this?"

"I want to see the sims get a fair shake."

He glanced at her card again. *Consultant* . . . to whom?

"Are you with one of those animal rights groups?"

"My interest is personal. So what's your decision, Mr. Patrick Sullivan, attorney at law?"

The subtle little twist she put on those last three words gave Patrick the impression that somehow she'd already guessed the answer.

"I haven't come to one yet."

She stared at him a moment, her expression frankly dubious. Then she put her briefcase on the table and released the catches.

"Very well. If you're sitting on the fence, perhaps this will tip you toward the sims."

She gave the briefcase a one-eighty swivel, lifted the top, and Patrick found himself nose to nose with more cash than he'd ever seen in one spot in his life—he'd handled bigger checks, sure, but this was *cash*.

Hoping his eyes weren't bugging, he lifted a packet and fanned it.

"All twenties, Mr. Sullivan."

"How—?" The words seemed to catch in his throat. "How many?"

"Exactly twelve-thousand, five hundred. To spare you doing the math, that's a quarter of a million dollars.

When I have your assurance that you will continue the fight, I will deposit it all into the sim legal defense fund."

Patrick eyed the money. This would take him a long way into the case; and with other contributions he could stir up during the proceedings, probably all the way through, with maybe a good chunk left over at the end.

Tempting . . . Jesus, it was tempting.

But staying with the sims meant being booted from the firm . . . going solo. He didn't care for that idea. Payes & Hecht could be a cutthroat place at times, but even on the worst days he found a certain level of comfort in having a firm behind him. Like a security blanket—one trimmed with barbed wire, perhaps, but still . . .

And where would he be after the sim case, whatever the outcome? Who'd be his future clients? Sims? Hardly.

Uh-uh. Tempting as that cash was, he wasn't going to commit professional seppuku for it. But he couldn't tell this beautiful woman that. Painfully he pulled his gaze away from the money and looked at her.

"I'll take that into consideration, Ms. Cadman."

"Good." She snapped the cover closed on all that beautiful green. "When do you expect to finalize your decision?"

"Before the end of the day."

"Wonderful."

One word . . . but the acid she managed to lace through it seared him to the core. She was looking right through him, and her eyes, the twist of her lips, everything in her body language radiated contempt.

"My number is on the card. Call me when you decide."

She turned and walked out, leaving him mired in a pool of dismay. A woman like that, you wanted her looking at you with admiration, not like something that had just crawled out from under a rock.

But what else was he supposed to do? What else *could* he do? Sometimes you simply had to be pragmatic.

Patrick sighed. The perfect cap on the worst weeks of his life.

He heard a patter behind him and turned toward the window. It had begun to rain. Hard. Great.

With his mood darker than the weather, Patrick stepped out into the hall. Off to his right he spotted the pretty lady with the briefcase full of pretty money waiting for the elevator.

"I'm going to grab a cup of coffee," he told Maggie.

"Want me to get it for you?" she said, looking up from her computer screen.

"Thanks, but you're busier than I am at the moment."

Down the hall, laughter echoed from the open doorway of the kitchenette that housed the coffee maker and a small refrigerator. He slowed his approach when he heard his name.

A voice he recognized as belonging to one of the younger associates was saying, ". . . and so when I *still* won't give Skipper steak instead of dog chow, he says, 'I'll get you! I'm calling Sim-Sim Sullivan!'"

More laughter. Patrick felt his face flush. Setting his jaw he turned and glanced back at the waiting area. The elevator doors were sliding open and Romy Cadman was stepping inside. He broke into a run.

"Ms. Cadman! Hold those doors!"

She turned and gave him a quizzical look, but put out a hand to stall the doors. He hopped into the cab beside her.

"I've made up my mind,' he told her.

She blinked, shock and disbelief playing tag across her features. "You mean—"

I know I'm going to regret this, he thought, but fuck 'em. Fuck 'em all.

"Damn right. Want to meet my clients?"

Her smile lit the elevator. "I'd love to."

3

Romy's head spun as she followed Sullivan's BMW through the downpour to the golf club.

What happened back there? she wondered. There he was, standing in his office, and he's clearly out of the picture—wouldn't say so to her face, but she'd seen defeat in his eyes, his posture, *I quit* written all over him—and a couple of minutes later he's jumping into the elevator with her and not looking back.

Had he truly been on the fence and she'd misread him? She'd been so *sure* . . .

Well, no use in beating it to death. He was still on board. That was what counted. She didn't know how good Sullivan was, but at least the sims still had a lawyer.

He stopped next to a high privet hedge and she pulled in behind him. She grabbed her umbrella and stepped out of her car. The umbrella was auto open which was good because she had the briefcase in her other hand. She had no intention of leaving it in the car.

An umbrellaless Sullivan came splashing over to her.

"Let me help," he said, reaching for the briefcase.

She handed him the umbrella handle. "Help with this."

"Aaawww," he said, grinning.

Nice smile. Gave him a boyish look. Like a mischievous child.

Together they sloshed through the soggy grass toward a barrack-like building.

"Most of the caddies and gardening sims should be in. Not a golf day. You'll have to come back at night after the kitchen and dining room close to catch all of them."

Patrick knocked and they were admitted by a grinning sim he introduced as Tome. Romy was prepared for the barrack, and her tours of the dorms prepared her for the vague musty odor that attended a crowd of sims. But she was totally unprepared for the reception.

Like Jesus's return to Jerusalem. Cheering, waving, jumping on furniture, and cries of "Mist Sulliman!" from a dozen sim throats. Everything short of throwing palm fronds at his feet.

Flushed and looking a little embarrassed, Sullivan turned and gave her a self-conscious shrug. "My clients."

"My God," she said, unable to hide her awe. "They . . . they love you."

A sheepish grin. "Yeah, well . . ."

"No. They truly do. How could you have ever even considered . . . ?"

His blue eyes widened, not in surprise that she'd guessed, but more in fear that she'd say it out loud. But she'd never do that—not to his sims. Everyone, even sims, needed someone or something to believe in, even if their god was made of tin.

And that need in these sims further bolstered her conviction that all sims were too close to human to be treated as they were . . . as property . . . as slaves.

"It's all very complicated," he said.

Romy shook her head. "No, it's not. It's all very simple, really: You do the right thing."

"But right for whom? What's good for the right hand may not necessarily be good for the left. In case you don't know, my specialty is labor relations. It's all negotiation. The art of the possible."

"You've got to draw a line somewhere."

He shook his head. "The client and the opposition draw the lines. Then I try to get them to move their lines to a place that both sides can live with."

"But these particular clients can't draw that line," she told him. "They don't know how, they wouldn't know where. So you've got to draw it for them, making certain it's in the right place. And then you've got to stand in front of that line and say, 'This far and no farther.' No matter what is thrown against you—SimGen, the Teamsters, the US Government: 'This far and no farther.'"

Now Sullivan's turn to shake his head. "It's all so clear and simple to you?"

"Crystal and absolutely."

The tumultuous greeting had run its course, but a second round of cheering followed when Sullivan introduced Romy and announced that she was contributing "lots of money" to pay for the legal battles ahead. That finally died down, and now the sim called Tome was leading a young female toward them.

"Mist Sulliman. Meet new sim. Anj."

Dressed in the bib overalls and T-shirt that seemed to be the off-duty uniform of the Beacon Ridge sims, Anj was young and slight—couldn't have weighed more than eighty pounds fully dressed—and clung shyly to Tome, not making eye contact. Romy put out her hand and Tome had to take Anj's arm and extend it for a handshake. But she needed no prompting to grasp Sullivan's. Even smiled.

"Tome tell Anj all 'bout Mist Sulliman," Tome said.

The gathering's attention shifted from the two humans to the food cart that was being wheeled in by a pair of kitchen sims.

"Lunch," said Tome. "You eat?"

They both declined and watched as Tome led Anj away.

"Seems awful young, doesn't she?" Sullivan said.

Romy was seething. "SimGen can't breed sims fast enough to meet demand, so they're leasing them out at younger and younger ages."

She watched them line up, plates in hand, for servings of some sort of stew being ladled out of a big pot with *SIMS* hand-printed in red on the side. A scuffle broke out between two of them when one tried to cut ahead in line. Tome had to leave Anj to break it up, and she stood alone, looking lost.

"It's criminal," Romy said.

Sullivan didn't seem too concerned. "Speaking of lunch, we need someplace to talk. How about—?"

"I had a big breakfast. How about right here?"

"Too crowded."

"They're busy eating," she said, gesturing to the sims seating themselves at the long tables. "Besides, I'm used to being around sims. I work for OPRR. I'm a field agent in its Division of Animal Welfare."

"Sounds government."

"Yes and no."

They found a couple of empty easy chairs angled toward each other and she explained how the Office for the Protection of Research Risks was part of the National Institutes of Health, indirectly funded by the government.

"Then that's government money?" he said, pointing to the briefcase. "I don't know if I'll be allowed to use—"

"*My* money, Mr. Sullivan," she replied, glad she could say that truthfully. "Mine. To do with as I wish, and this happens to be what I wish. But I want a commitment from you, Mr. Sullivan."

"Only judges and opposing attorneys call me Mr. Sullivan. Makes me feel like I'm in court. Can you call me Patrick, please?"

And if I do, she thought, looking at him, I suppose I'm going to have to tell you to call me Romy. First names make us sound like friends. Do I want to sound like your friend, Patrick Sullivan? Can I trust you enough?

"Maybe when we know each other better . . . when I see how much of a commitment you have to this project. I'm more interested in commitment than first names, Mr. Sullivan."

"I—"

At that moment Anj appeared at his side and crawled into his chair.

"Um, uh . . . hello, Anj," he said, looking nonplused and not a little uncomfortable. "Can I help you?"

The young sim said nothing as she draped herself across his lap, then curled up and began sucking her thumb. She looked so small and fragile in those baggy overalls.

"Too young," Romy said, feeling her anger begin to cook again. "They're sending them out too damn young."

Sullivan sat stiff as a board in his easy chair. "What's she doing?"

Romy noticed Anj's eyelids drooping. "Looks like she's going to take a nap."

"Great. And what do I do while she's catching Z's?"

"Just sit there while we finish our discussion," Romy said, not particularly liking herself for the enjoyment she was taking in his discomfiture. "Commitment, remember?"

"You're going to make me sick of that word."

"I won't need to mention it again if I get it from you."

"Commitment how?"

"That you'll devote enough of your professional time to the sims to see that they get a fair shake."

"Time?" he said, eyebrows rising. "You want time, you got it. As of today I'm quitting Payes & Hecht to devote myself full time to these guys."

Romy couldn't help but wonder if Sullivan was quitting his firm or his firm was quitting him. No matter. Either way he'd have only one client.

"Excellent, Mr. Sullivan. I'll deposit the money this afternoon."

"It's going to be a long, bumpy road," he said. He gestured around at the barrack. "I mean, let's face it: this isn't a bad life. Sims have it pretty good, don't you think?"

"These sims, maybe, but they're a lucky minority. You can't imagine what I've seen. As a matter of fact..."

She stopped herself. Did she dare? Yes. Why not? Mr. Patrick Sullivan needed something to rile him up, stiffen his spine.

"Tell you what," she said. "I'll call you in the next day or two and bring you along as I wind up an investigation I've been pursuing for weeks. You game?"

He shrugged. "Sure. I'll just need—"

Anj whimpered. Her eyes were closed in her sleep.

"Misses her mother, I'll bet," Romy said.

Sullivan stared down at the young sim. "Afraid I can't help her there."

"Want me to take her?"

He raised a hand and gingerly, gently, began stroking her stiff, stringy hair. "No. That's all right."

And Romy realized she was catching a glimpse of a facet of Patrick Sullivan that he hid from the world, perhaps even from himself.

"You prefer Patrick to Pat?" she said.

He glanced up with a surprised expression, then grimaced. "Pat was that mystery-gender person on *Saturday Night Live*. And Patty makes me sound like I should be holding up the bar at the Dublin House Pub. Just Patrick."

"All right, Patrick," she said. She hesitated, then figured, what the hell. "And you might as well call me Romy."

He grinned and they sat and talked about things other than sims while Anj napped.

4

Sussex County, NJ

"Sullivan quit the firm rather than drop the sims!"
Mercer Sinclair said.

He pushed his chair back from his desk and began to
pace his office. The news had reached him this morning
and immediately he'd called Voss and Portero. Somehow
his brother had got wind of it and showed up as well. Not
that Ellis would contribute anything. Not that Mercer
cared. He was too baffled, too pissed to care.

"I can't believe it!" he went on. "Is the man crazy?
Has he suddenly become a crusader? What's gotten into
him?"

Able Voss cleared his throat. "An infusion of cash,
it appears."

"Really? How much?"

"Quarter mil."

Mercer was stunned. "A quarter—who'd give that
kind of money to a small town ambulance chaser?"

"That boy's no rube. He was ready and waitin with an injunction when Beacon Ridge tried to trade some of its sims to another club. And he had another ready in record time when we issued that recall on them. He's anticipated us at every turn. He may be an opportunist, but he's a smart one."

"Fine. He got lucky. But where did the money come from?"

"A cashier's check," Voss said. "That's all I know."

"Perfect," Mercer said, cracking his knuckles in frustration. "So we can't trace it."

"Yes, we can," Portero said, speaking for the first time. "Any transaction over ten thousand has to be reported."

Of course, Mercer thought. He should have remembered that.

He stared at the security chief, standing there in his dark suit with his hands tucked behind his back, straight as a board, like some parade ground tin soldier waiting to be inspected.

"Then let's do it!"

"It's done."

"Already?"

"My people have been monitoring the defense fund."

My people . . . Mercer knew Portero didn't mean the SimGen security department he headed. His *people*—no one referred to them by name—were elsewhere, far off the SimGen campus, and Mercer wasn't the least bit surprised that they'd devoted a small part of their vast resources to keeping an eye on Patrick Sullivan's activities.

He shivered ever so slightly at the thought of being the object of their cold scrutiny.

"Why didn't you say so in the first place?"

Mercer thought he sensed an instant of hesitation in Portero but couldn't be sure. He doubted this man had an uncertain cell in his body . . . and yet, he'd seen something flash across his face.

"We are looking into an unexpected aspect of the situation."

"Which is?"

"The purchaser of the cashier's check was a Ms. Romy Cadman. You may remember the name: She led the OPRR inspection team."

Mercer stiffened. "OPRR? You don't think—?"

Voss shook his head. "OPRR's budget just barely covers its expenses. Even if it had the surplus it wouldn't jeopardize its funding by getting involved in something like this."

"Is she independently wealthy?" Mercer said, feeling his unease growing by the minute. "Where'd she get that kind of money?"

"She lives modestly on a modest income," Portero said flatly. "She purchased the check with cash. That is all we know—so far."

A quarter of a million in cash. And probably more where that came from. Someone out there wanted Sullivan to succeed.

Again that sense of malevolent convergence through which he could almost hear the gears of some giant piece of machinery starting to turn . . . an engine of destruction. But whose engine? Whose destruction?

"I don't like this," Mercer said.

"Neither do my people," Portero said. "We're going to handle matters from here."

"Meaning what?" Ellis said.

Mercer glanced at his brother. Their eyes met. On this they could agree; neither of them were comfortable with the way Portero's people handled problems.

"Meaning this situation is spinning out of control. Your attempt to stop Sullivan failed. Now it's our turn."

"Now wait a minute," Voss said, both chins jiggling as he hauled his bulk out of the chair. "Wait just one damn minute. Don't you folks say another word until I'm on the right side of that door. I don't need to hear this."

He hustled across the gray carpet and let himself out.

As soon as the door closed Ellis turned to Portero. "You're not planning to—"

"No plans have been finalized, but direct action will be taken."

"No!" Ellis said, rising. "I'm not going to sit by while you and your people pull more of your dirty tricks."

"You have no choice, I'm afraid," Portero said without changing his inflection. "The matter is out of your hands. Sullivan has proven smarter and more stubborn than anyone anticipated. Even though the chance that his suit will set a precedent is remote, the mere possibility that he might succeed is unacceptable. It has been decided to stop him now, before he uses the courtroom to plant himself in the national consciousness."

"My God!" Ellis moaned, shutting his eyes. "Why did we ever become involved with you?"

Portero didn't answer. No answer was needed. But here again, for the second time in as many minutes—a rare occurrence, to be sure—Mercer could agree with his brother. He wished at times like these that they'd found another way to finance their start-up back in the seventies. But he knew that later, when he'd settled down and was able to regain his perspective, the feeling would pass, and once again he'd appreciate how SimGen never could have achieved its current dominance without the help of the people behind Portero.

Portero said, "We also intend to learn the source of the Cadman woman's money."

"How will you do that?"

"Not your concern." And again a flash of something in Portero's ebony eyes, almost like regret this time. "But we will know."

5

Sussex County, NJ

"You're not getting another beer, are you?" Martha called from the upstairs bedroom.

Harry Carstairs stood before his open refrigerator, marveling at the acuity of his wife's hearing.

"Just one more."

"Harry!" She drew out the second syllable. "Haven't you had enough for one night?"

No, he thought. Not yet.

"It's just a light."

"Aren't you ever coming to bed?"

"Soon, hon."

She grumbled something he didn't catch and he could visualize her rolling onto her side and pulling the covers over her head. He twisted the cap off the beer, took a quick pull, then stepped over to the bar. There he gently lifted the Seagram's bottle and poured a good slug into his beer.

Gently swirling the mixture, he headed for his study at the other end of the house.

He was drinking too much, he knew. But it took a lot of booze to put a dent in a guy his size. Still he didn't think it was a real problem. He didn't drink during the day, didn't even think about it when he was surrounded by his hordes of young sims. Their rambunctious energy recharged him every morning, filling his mind and senses all day.

But when he got home, when it was just Martha and he, the charge drained away, leaving him empty and flat. A dead battery. Not that there was anything wrong with Martha. Not her fault. It was all him.

He wished now they'd had kids. Life had been so fine before when it was just the two of them. And SimGen, of course. Martha worked for the company too, in the comptroller's office. SimGen had moved into their house, turning their marriage into a ménage à trois. But it had been a rewarding arrangement. They'd built their dream house on this huge wooded lot, traveled extensively, and had two fat 401(k)s that would allow them comfortable early retirement if they wanted it.

But four years ago he'd begun to feel an aching emptiness here, to sense the isolation of the surrounding woods. He knew the day, the hour, the moment it had begun: When Ellis Sinclair had informed him about the sudden death of a sim.

Not just any sim. A special sim, one Ellis had known throughout his entire time at SimGen. He'd taught that sim chess and turned him into a damn good player. They used to play three or four times a week.

And then he was gone. Just like that. Died on a Saturday, into the crematorium on Sunday, and his quarters stripped by the time Harry returned to work on Monday morning.

The boilermakers—Martha thought they were just plain beers—numbed the ache. But the ache seemed to require more anesthetic with each passing year.

Harry settled himself at his desk and was about to restart the computer chess match he'd paused in mid game when—

He stopped. That feeling again. A prickling along his scalp . . . as if he was being watched.

Harry abruptly swiveled his chair toward the window directly behind him and caught a glimpse of a pale blur ducking out of sight. He sat stunned, frozen with the knowledge that he hadn't been imagining it. Someone had been watching him through that goddamn window!

He leaped from his seat, lumbering toward the sliding glass doors that opened from his study onto the rear deck. He slipped, fell to one knee—damn boilermakers!—then yanked back the door and lurched onto the deck.

"I saw you, damn it!" he shouted, voice echoing through the trees, breath fogging in the cold air. "Who are you? Who the *fuck* are you!"

He stopped, listening. Where'd he go? But the woods were silent.

And then Martha's voice, frightened, crying: "Harry! Harry, come quick!"

Harry ran back inside, charging the length of the house, shouting her name. He made it up the stairs to the master bedroom where he found her standing in the dark, staring out the big window overlooking the front yard.

45

"What is it?"

"I saw someone out there!" Her hand fluttered before her mouth like a hummingbird over a flower. "Just a glimpse. He was moving away toward the road but I know I saw him!"

"*Now* do you believe me?"

He'd told her before about this feeling of being watched but Martha had always chalked it up to his drinking.

"Yes! Yes, I do! And I'm calling the police!"

"Good. You do that," Harry said, feeling a deep rage start to burn—damn, it was good to feel something again. He headed for the stairs. "And tell them to hurry. Because if I get to him first they'll have to scrape what's left of him into a goddamn bucket!"

"Harry, no!" Martha cried.

Harry ignored her. His blood was up, he could feel it racing through his head, his muscles. He'd been spooked, he'd been doubted, he'd even doubted himself, but now it was clear he'd been right all along and it was time for a little payback, time to kick some major donkey.

He hit the front drive running and sprinted for the street. In seconds his heart was thudding, his lungs burning.

Out of shape. And four sheets to the wind. But he was going to catch this fucker, and before he wiped up the road with him, he was going to find out why he—

Ahead . . . to the right . . . a car engine turning over, gears engaging, tires squealing on pavement.

Shit!

By the time Harry reached the street all he could see was a distant pair of tail lights shrinking into the darkness.

46

He bent, hands on thighs, grunting and gasping for air. Maybe it was for the best. If he had caught up with the guy he might have been too winded to do much more than grab him and fall on him and hope he crushed the fucking hell out of him.

But the worst part was he still had no answers. Why was somebody watching him? Why should anyone care enough about him to come out here and sit in the cold dark woods to watch him play chess with his computer.

Get a life, man!

One thing was certain—no, make that two . . . two things were certain.

First, he was going to get a gun. Tomorrow.

Second, he was going to stop drinking. At least stop drinking so much. Also tomorrow.

Right now he was thoroughly rattled and needed a double of something. Anything. Just so long as it was a double.

6

New York City

"There it is," Romy said, pointing.

Patrick squinted down the garbage-strewn alley to where a naked bulb glowed dimly above a dented metal door. Back in the Roaring Twenties, a speakeasy might have hid behind a door like that. Here in the twenty-first century he knew nothing so innocuous awaited him.

"I don't like this."

A week had passed since she'd barreled into his life. She'd called him this afternoon, suggesting they meet in the city for a late dinner, and then she wanted to show him a few sights.

So after an excellent meal in the Flatiron district, with perhaps a little too much wine, she'd cabbed him down to this crummy ill-lit neighborhood in the west teens, so far west he could smell the river.

He felt like a fish out of water: overdressed and under leathered. Romy's long black leather coat matched the dominant color of the passing locals, but Patrick's white shirt, paisley tie, and herringbone overcoat made him stand out like a Klansman at a NAACP meeting.

"Nothing to worry about," she said.

"Easy for you to say. You're staying out here."

He glanced around uneasily. He was no country boy, knew Manhattan pretty well, in fact; but this was a part of the city he tended to avoid. Clubs down here were in the news too often, usually connected to stories about shootings and drug overdoses.

Romy's smile had a bitter twist. "I'd go in with you, but it's not exactly my kind of place."

"You keep saying that, but it doesn't help me. Before I walk in there I'd much rather know whose kind of place it *is* than whose kind it isn't."

"You need to find out for yourself."

"Okay then, why don't I find out in the daytime?"

"Because the action at a place like this doesn't get rolling until about now."

"This is all because I said I thought sims had a pretty cushy existence, right?"

"Stop stalling," she said, giving him a gentle punch on the shoulder. "Are you going to knock on that door or not?"

Patrick tried a grin. "I'd love to except that it means leaving you out here alone on these mean streets."

"Oh, I can take care of myself," she said, and this time her smile had a touch of warmth in it.

"Okay," he said. "Here I go."

He walked the dozen or so paces to the door, took a deep breath of urine-tinged air, and rapped on its battered, flaking surface.

A narrow window slid open and two dark eyes peered out at him.

"Yeah?" said a harsh voice.

Feeling as if he'd stepped into a particularly corny episode of the old *Untouchables*, he said, "I'd, um, like to come in."

"Ever been here before?"

"No, um, a bartender at The Tunnel sent me."

"What's his name?"

"Tim. He told me to tell you that Tim sent me."

Actually, Patrick had never met Tim, but Romy had told him to say that.

The door opened. Fighting the urge to turn and trot back down the alley, he stepped inside. The door slammed shut behind him and Patrick found himself sharing a long narrow hallway with a two-legged slab of beef who probably held graduate degrees in bar bouncing: shaved head, earrings, crooked nose, and a steroidal body stuffed into a sleeveless black T-shirt emblazoned with "Mother's." An old Guns n' Roses tune vibrated from the end of the hall.

The slab held out his hand. "Twenty-five bucks."

"What for?"

"Door charge."

"Twenty-five bucks just to walk in?"

"You see busloads of gooks marchin through here? This ain't no sightseeing stop. Pay up or walk."

Patrick reached into his pocket. "Tim didn't say anything about a door charge."

"He's not supposed to." The bouncer grinned and stuck out his tongue—long and forked—and waggled it in Patrick's face.

51

A splicer, Patrick thought, trying to hide his revulsion. What the hell has Romy got me into?

Patrick handed him the money.

"Welcome to the Jungle." The bouncer pointed toward the end of the hall. "Mona will take care of you," he said, then cupped his hands around his mouth and shouted, "Incoming! Newbie!"

Patrick hurried down the hallway, brushing the sides in his haste. The faster he went, the sooner this would be over. He hoped.

Mona—at least he assumed the obese woman in the tight red dress exposing acres of cleavage was Mona—met him at the end of the hall. Another splicer: oversized lizard scales ran up the sides of her face and across her throat and who knew where else. She and the bouncer must be a couple—both into reptiles.

He remembered when tattoos and piercing were considered avant garde, but eventually they'd been mainstreamed. Then tailored genes and non-human splices hit the black market and the bod-mod crowd jumped on them like cats on a nip-coated mouse.

"Hi, honey," she said, showing pointed teeth in a big welcoming grin. "First time, huh?"

"Uh, yeah."

First time for *what*?

"Everybody's a little nervous the first time." She took his arm and led him around a corner. "Let me introduce you to the girls first, then you take your time and pick the one you want. The base charge is two-fifty and that allows you half an hour. We charge extra if you go over, and of course there's surcharges for any specialties you want . . ."

Patrick stopped cold when he saw them.

"Kinda gets you, don't it," Mona said. "Nobody ever imagines they could look this good."

The "girls" were female sims, but nothing like Patrick had ever seen or imagined. Someone had caked them with makeup, either styled and dyed their hair or fitted them with wigs, then dressed them in vinyl or studded leather or lingerie—satin teddies, frilly see-through nighties, the whole Frederick's of Hollywood catalog. And their legs—most of them had shaved legs. Sims as a rule were only slightly hairier than humans, and the hair was coarser, but they didn't shave their legs or underarms. Patrick had never seen a shaved female sim, or ones with such breasts—they must have had implants.

"Good Christ!" he blurted. "What have you done to them?"

He did his best to hide his revulsion as Mona gave him a sharp look, but God it wasn't easy. Sim whores....

She grinned again and gave him a knowing wink. "You don't like them all dolled up? That's all right. I think I know your type."

"You do?" That possibility was almost as unsettling as the sight of these sim sex slaves.

She pointed to two unshaven, unenhanced females lounging nude on a couch.

"We've got Teen and Mone over there. They work in our special jungle room for our clients who like their sims just the way you'd encounter them in the wild."

"In the wild? They don't *occur* in the wild! They're . . . manufactured!"

"Hey," Mona said, her smile fading. "Are you here to have fun or nit-pick my ass?"

Patrick stared, he gawked, he gaped in shock at their surreal sicko get-ups. His stupefaction that anyone could find these pathetic creatures even remotely erotic quickly faded, replaced by a deeper revulsion as he noticed the bruises on their shaved limbs, their dead dull eyes. They looked like desiccated shells as they sat and smoked and stared at him.

Smoked . . . he'd never known a sim to smoke.

He had to get out of here. Now.

"I . . . I think I've changed my mind."

"What's the matter?" She looked genuinely offended. "We got the best in town."

Patrick started backing toward the hallway. "I'm sure you do, it's just that I . . . nothing personal, but I don't think I'm ready yet."

Glaring now, Mona said, "Then why'd you come?"

"A friend told me to." God, he wanted to kill Romy. "Said I'd find it enlightening. But I don't."

He turned and headed for the door where the bouncer waited.

"Jerry!" Mona called out behind him. "Something's not right with this guy."

Jerry placed himself between Patrick and the door.

"You got a problem, pal?"

Oh, no, Patrick thought. He's going to beat the shit out of me.

"Yeah," Patrick said, pressing one hand against his stomach and the other over his mouth. "I think I'm going to be sick." He retched for effect.

"Don't you even fuckin dream of it, asshole! You puke in here, you're gonna clean it up—with your tongue!"

Patrick retched again, louder this time. "Oh, God!" He doubled over.

"Motherf—"

He felt the back of his suit coat bunch as Jerry grabbed a fistful of fabric, heard the door swing open, and then he was propelled into the stink of the alley. He stumbled, almost lost his footing, but managed to stay upright as he skidded to a halt against the brick wall on the far side.

Patrick didn't stop to look back. He pushed off the wall and hurried from the alley at something just short of a trot. He found Romy waiting for him on the sidewalk.

"Well?" she said, raising her eyebrows.

"Damn you."

He'd half expected some sort of ha-ha-the-joke's-on-you attitude, but she was all business.

"I take it you ran into a few sims."

"You know damn well I did!" God, he was pissed. He felt besmirched, belittled, diminished. If she'd been a guy he'd be taking a poke at her right now. "Why the hell—?"

She held up one hand to silence him and raised the other to her lips. He realized she was holding a cell phone.

"My man inside confirms the sims are there. It's a go."

"What's a go?" Patrick said.

"A raid," she said. "Let's get out of the way."

She led him across the street. The first blue and white NYPD units were screeching to a halt in front of the alley by the time they reached the opposite curb. Patrick watched fascinated as a small horde of blue uniforms swarmed down the alley.

Patrick stared at Romy. "You're a cop?"

"No. And this sort of work isn't really a kosher part of my OPRR duties, but I've made it so. I snoop around. I talk to people, people talk to me. I've been watching this place for a while. Took me better than a week to find the rear exit. Once I had that, I brought in NYPD."

"Then what did you need me for? Why'd you send me in there?"

Her gaze was focused on the alley, her onyx eyes hard and bright as she watched the cops knock open the door with a battering ram.

"To make sure the sims were inside. You never know who's got a source in a precinct house. If they got wind of the raid they'd have the sims stashed out of town and I'd have egg on my face and the cops would be less cooperative next time I came to them with a sim violation."

If she thought that was going to mollify him, she was dead wrong.

"You could have told me, damn it! Why'd you send me in there with no idea what I'd be getting into?"

"Would you have gone in if I had?"

"Well . . ." He let the word trail off but knew the answer would have been a definite no.

"I didn't think so. But because you did, you played a meaningful part in reeling in some single-celled organisms posing as human beings, *things*"—she managed to inject so much contempt into the word—"who make pond scum look tasty." A wry smile. "Ain't that cool?"

Patrick had to admit it was, but wasn't about to say so.

"What happens to them?"

"The humans won't see daylight for a long, long time. Those sims in there have been either abducted or leased under false pretenses. The charges will range from grand theft to fraud to pandering to cruelty to animals to operating a criminal enterprise to promoting bestiality and whatever else the prosecutors can think of. You're the lawyer. You can imagine."

Patrick nodded, mentally adding a few more charges.

Romy kept talking. "And the perps—do I sound like a cop?—are guaranteed to get slammed with max sentences. SimGen, as you've learned firsthand, is relentless when it comes to anyone messing with their product. Their contacts in the judicial system, the ones who manage to guarantee them favorable rulings whenever necessary, also see to it that anyone who transgresses against them lands lower-lip deep in doo-doo. And after the criminal courts are through with the bastards, SimGen chases them down in civil court and gets dibs on everything they've ever owned in their life and everything they'll earn till Resurrection Day."

"You sound almost . . . admiring."

Romy shook her head. "Not admiration. But you've got to respect SimGen's efficiency. When their ends coincide with mine—as in rescuing sims from these oxygen wasters—I'm only too happy to take advantage of that efficiency. But we part on the *why*: my reasons are personal and ethical, theirs are purely business and public relations."

"What happens to the sims?" he said, remembering the tarted-up females.

"Someone from SimGen will be by to pick up the poor things and take them to the Jersey campus where they'll rehab the ones they can and retire the ones they can't."

"Doesn't exactly sound like the Evil Empire to me."

She turned and glared at him. "Oh, but they are, Patrick Sullivan. That sleazy little operation across the street couldn't have existed without SimGen, because SimGen made the sims that were mistreated in there."

"Hey, Ford makes cars and some people get drunk and kill people with them or use them to rob banks or rig them with dynamite."

She rolled her eyes. "You don't see the difference between a hunk of tin and those creatures you're representing in court?"

"Of course I do. I just—"

"SimGen created a new species and enslaved it. Sims feel pain, they feel pleasure, they laugh, they *think*, damn it! And they're slaves. A slave species . . . you don't think that's evil?"

"Well, when you put it that way . . . "

"What other way is there to put it? They've got to be stopped."

Patrick laughed. "And who's going to do that? You?"

She nodded. "Yes."

He couldn't believe this. She actually seemed serious. "You don't really think—"

"Something's rotten in SimGen," she said. "They're dirty. When I was there I could smell it. And when I find out what they're hiding, I'm going to bring them down."

"You."

She set her jaw. "Me . . . with a little help from some friends."

"What friends?"

"Just . . . friends." She stepped off the curb. "I'm going in to check over those sims, catalogue any injuries or evidence of drugging before the SimGen folks arrive. Want to come along?"

Patrick hesitated. He'd already been inside once and wasn't keen on going back.

"I don't know . . . I've got an early day tomorrow..."

"I know. Beacon Ridge has filed some new motions on the federal appeal."

That gave him a mild jolt. "You're really staying on top of this, aren't you."

"I tend to keep a close eye on my investments. As a matter of fact, I was planning on coming up to White Plains tomorrow."

"What for?"

"To see you in action."

"Ah, yes. Your investment." He wasn't sure if he liked the idea. He wasn't some trick pony.

"If you hang around awhile you could give me a ride up there."

Now *here* was an interesting development. "Where are you staying?"

"Don't know yet. How's your motel?"

Whoa! His heart did a pole vault. "Not fancy, but decent. As a matter of fact, you could save yourself a few bucks and stay in my room."

She laughed from deep in her throat. God, what a sound. He could listen to her laugh all night. Visions of that marvelous tight body began to play in his head . . . in bed next to him, straddling him . . . Pamela had been gone for too long and right now every Y-chromosome in his body was doing a mating dance.

"I don't think so."

He raised his hands. "Nothing salacious here. The room's got two double beds. You could have the other one."

"How generous," she said with a wry twist to her smile. "And I appreciate the offer, but I'm a private sort of person. But you will drive me?"

Drive you . . . aw, lady, don't say things like that.

"Sure."

"Great. We'll have to stop at my office to pick up my overnight bag."

"No problem."

And on the way home, lady, I'm going to do my absolute damnedest to convince you that the two of us renting two rooms is one too many.

7

Westchester County

Romy glanced at the clock numerals glowing on the dashboard of Patrick's car. Hard to believe it was quarter to three already.

Time flies when you're having fun.

Well, not fun, exactly. But it had been a good night. And she felt *very* good about putting those sim abusers behind bars.

She watched Patrick as he maneuvered the car along the winding curves of the Saw Mill River Parkway, deserted at this hour except for the single pair of headlights a couple of hundred yards behind them. He'd handled himself well tonight. And she'd been heartened by how deeply the sim bordello had shaken him.

"Tired?" she said.

"A little. How about you?"

"Not a bit." That was a fact: she was totally wired.

"I could perk up," he said with a grin. "That is, if you decide to take up my offer on the sleeping arrangements."

She laughed. "You don't give up, do you."

After the splicer slimeballs had been carted off, and SimGen had picked up the sims, and the cops had returned to Manhattan South, they'd retrieved his car from the garage, picked up her bag, and headed for the northern suburbs. Patrick had spent most of the trip on the make, pitching his idea of sharing a room. Finally he seemed to have run out of gas.

Romy had to admit that a bout of sweaty, energetic sex would be perfect right now. Might take the edge off this persistent adrenaline buzz. But not with Patrick Sullivan. They'd be working too closely over the next few months. That level of intimacy in their relationship would further complicate an already complicated situation.

"If you're half this tenacious on behalf of your clients, I don't think the sims can lose."

"As me grandma used to say," he said in a pretty fair Irish accent, "from yer lips to Gawd's ear."

"Still think all sims have it cushy?" she said.

"Not those."

"And they didn't have it a tenth as bad as some of the cases I've seen. Try to imagine a sim tossed into a ring with three pit bulls."

"Aw no."

"Or two sims shoved into a pit, knives duct-taped into both hands, and bullwhipped until they fight to the death."

"Stop!"

"And some are simply tied up in a basement and tortured for days, weeks."

"Christ, Romy, *please!*"

She'd seen too much, too damn much over the years. Tears welled in her eyes.

"I don't know why . . . maybe it's because they're so unassertive, or because they have no franchise, but sims seem to bring out the very worst in the worst of us. The racists who're so desperate to feel superior to something, anything, even if it's not human; others who think God gave them the animal kingdom as their playground, to do absolutely anything with that they damn well please; and the sick souls who want to vent their psychoses on something weak and defenseless. Serial killers, teenage gangs, they've found a new target: kill a sim for kicks. Damn them." She heard her voice break. "Damn them all to hell."

"Easy," Patrick said, reaching across, finding her hand, squeezing it. "Easy."

Romy couldn't gauge the genuineness of the gesture, whether he really felt for her or was simply pressing his case to be roommates, but she didn't pull away.

The interior of the car brightened. Romy glanced in her sideview mirror and saw that the car behind them was closer now, coming up fast. Patrick noticed it too.

"Looks like someone wants to pass," he said.

She felt the BMW decelerate as Patrick eased up on the gas to allow the other car to go by. She looked out her window at the ravine beyond the guardrail, and suddenly she had a premonition.

"Don't slow down!" she cried.

"Wha?"

"Hit the gas! Don't let it pass!"

Too late. The other car had gained too much momentum. It pulled alongside—Romy could see now that it was a big, heavy Chevy van—and then cut a hard right into the Beamer's flank. Patrick cried out and the car swerved as he was knocked away from the steering wheel. Metal screeched, sparks flew as they ripped along the steel guardrail. Patrick grabbed the wheel, trying to regain control, but then the van hit them again, harder, and this time the Beamer climbed the guardrail, straddled it for an endless instant, then toppled over.

Romy's window exploded inward as the car landed on its passenger side—she heard someone screaming and recognized the voice as her own. The Beamer rolled onto its roof, then over to the driver side where it slid-bounced-rattled the rest of the way down a slope of softball-size chunks of granite until it hit the bottom of the ravine and bounced back onto its wheels.

She heard Patrick groaning and she thought, We're alive! But that was no accident! Someone tried to kill us!

And then she saw forms moving into the beam of the one remaining headlight, crouching forms in dark jumpsuits, looking like commandos.

Realization stabbed into her brain: Already down here! Waiting for us! All planned! We were supposed to be knocked off the road at that point!

She found the door lock toggle, hit it. Locks wouldn't do much good, but Patrick's window, though cracked, was still intact. She leaned close to him.

"Don't move!" she whispered in his ear.

He gave her a groggy look. "What?"

"Keep quiet and play dead!"

She pushed his head down so it was resting against the steering wheel, then slumped herself against him and watched through narrowed lids.

Three of them, moving quickly and cautiously, squinting in the light. Must have been waiting in the dark for a while. She thought she spotted a fourth figure hanging back at the edge of the glow.

Romy slipped her hand into her pocketbook, searching for something, anything she might use to protect herself. Her fingers closed around a metal cylinder, twice the length of a lipstick. Oh, yes. She'd all but forgotten about that.

"Somebody kill those lights!" said the middle figure.

"Got it."

One figure veered toward Patrick's side of the car while the other two approached Romy's. A hand snaked through her window. She steeled herself as fingers probed her throat.

"Got a pulse."

"Great. Get her arm out here. I'll shoot her up. Got that recorder ready?"

The third man was rattling Patrick's door. "Hey, it's locked. Find the switch over there."

A hand fumbled along the inside of her door. Over one man's shoulder she saw another lift a syringe.

No!

As soon as she heard the door locks trip open, she began spraying. Not a five- or ten-percent capsicum spray, but a concentrated stream of CS tear gas. The nearer of the two caught the full brunt of it. Clawing at his eyes, he cried out and lurched backward, knocking into his partner, and Romy was moving too, pushing open her door and leaping out, arm extended, giving the syringe man a faceful. He shouted and, arms across his face, turned and tried to run blind, but tripped and fell over the first guy.

"What the fuck?" she heard the third man say from Patrick's side of the car. She turned and saw him start to move around toward her.

"Run, Patrick!" she screamed. "Run now!"

Then she took her own advice, but not before giving each of these two bastards on the ground a couple of quick hard boots where they lived.

8

Patrick lay trembling against the steering wheel, trying to control his bladder, afraid he was going to be killed. The guy on his side of the car had just yanked the door open when all hell broke loose to Patrick's right—shouts, cries, moans, and then Romy telling him to run. The guy outside his door was moving away and so Patrick kicked the door the rest of the way open and did just that.

He didn't pick a direction, he simply ran with everything he had. A quick glance over his shoulder showed no one in pursuit, and a slim figure, glints of light flashing from her glossy leather coat, fading into the night on the far side of the car. Romy. Thank God.

He ran on, still afraid for his life, but he had a chance now, and that left room enough in his panicked brain for questions: Who? Why? And room for shame. He was running instead of fighting. Even though he wasn't a Claude Van Damme, or even close, he felt he should be back there defending Romy. Instead, she'd taken the lead and sprung them both. What kind of a woman had he become involved with?

At least they were running in opposite directions. That would split the opposition.

He spotted a large dark splotch ahead to his right—a tiny grove of trees, tall bushes maybe—and headed for it. He could stop there, get his bearings, and then try to make it back up to the road.

As he entered the grove he had a vague impression of a shadow hugging one of the dark tree trunks immediately to his right, but he kept pushing into the foliage.

"Not so fast, little man," said a deep voice.

And then something rammed into his abdomen, a fist, plunging toward his spine, almost reaching it. As Patrick grunted in airless agony and doubled over, another fist slammed into the back of his neck, collapsing him to his knees. He retched.

"Got him!" the voice bellowed.

Through the red and black splotches flashing in his vision, Patrick was aware of a flashlight flicking on and off. A moment later he heard thumping footsteps approach.

"Ricker?" said a voice that belonged to the guy who'd opened his car door.

"Over here. Where's Hoop and Cruz?"

As Patrick's breathing eased and his head cleared, he glanced left and right: two pairs of identical black sneakers leading to black pants with elastic cuffs.

"Down. Bitch was playing possum. Maced them and took off. They're getting their eyes back but—"

"Damn fuck better! Got to catch her before she gets to the road and stops a car!"

"That might be up to me and you—she did some real damage to their balls before she left."

"Shit! All right, let's do this guy, dump him back in his car, and go after her."

Do? Panic clawed at his brain. Did that mean what he thought?

For the second time tonight, Patrick felt himself grabbed by the back of his suit coat. This time he was hauled to his feet.

"Steady him," the big one, the one called Ricker said as Patrick felt a pair of massive arms twine around his head and neck like an anaconda.

"Wh-what're you doing?" he cried, although he sensed with a sick terrifying certainty what was coming.

"What the accident didn't, buddy-boy," said Ricker's voice close to his ear.

Patrick writhed in their grasp and cried out his mortal fear as he felt those arms tighten, but he was trapped and pinned and as utterly helpless as a moth about to have its wings plucked . . .

. . . and then a jarring impact, an agonized "Uhnh!" from Ricker, a startled "What the—?" from the other, and the murderous grip loosened, the arms fell away, and something slammed against Patrick's back, knocking him face first onto the ground. He heard scuffling feet, grunted as someone's heel kicked him in the ribs, then winced as he heard a loud, wet, crunching *smack!* followed by a brief light rain of warm heavy droplets against his head and the back of his neck. After that, a heartbeat of silence, followed by the impacts of two heavy objects thudding to the ground, one on his left, another on his right. Then . . .

. . . silence.

He waited in panicked confusion, holding his breath, playing dead, praying he'd survive the night. Silence persisted. Warily he raised his head, inching it upward, spitting the dirt from his lips. To his left he saw a pair of black-clad legs and sneakered feet, only this time they were horizontal. With growing alarm he slowly rotated his head left—

—and scrambled to his feet with a startled cry when he found a bloodstained face and dead staring eyes only inches from his own.

Heart hammering, he backed away from the two still forms, the one who'd been struggling with his car door, and the bigger one, the one called Ricker, the one who'd been about to snap his neck when—

When what? What had just happened here?

He did a full, stumbling turn as he edged out of the grove, searching the shadows for something, anything that might account for the two dead men, but found only more shadows. When he reached the edge of the foliage he ran, blindly at first, but then a passing splash of light from above told him where the roadway was. He veered right and began to claw his way up the steep slope, stumbling, slipping, the rough granite stones tearing his suit pants, cutting his skin. Finally he reached the steel guardrail and pulled himself over.

Aching and bleeding, he slumped against the cold metal and he tried to catch his breath.

Not in shape, he thought as he searched his pockets for his cell phone.

And even if he were, he wasn't in shape for a car jacking and dead bodies. He was a talker, not a fighter. He—

Shit! He'd plugged the phone into the recharger in the car!

All right. As soon as he claimed a second wind, he was going to start running, and keep on running until a car showed up. And then he was going to stop it and have them call 911.

Lights glowed beyond the curve to his left. As a car careened into view, he rose and staggered across the shoulder toward the roadway, waving his arms. Only when he was completely exposed and vulnerable did it occur to him to wonder whether it might be friend or foe.

No matter. The car hurtled past without even slowing.

Patrick looked down at his wrinkled, torn, bloodstained suit. *I wouldn't pick me up either.*

Maybe he'd be lucky and the driver would call in about a disheveled crazy-looking man wandering the Saw Mill. But the way his luck was running . . .

He ducked and turned as he heard a noise on the slope below . . . moving closer. Someone climbing his way. He peeked over the guardrail and sighed with relief when he recognized her.

"Romy!" he said, rising and extending his hand. "Thank God you're safe!"

And please don't say *No thanks to you, my hero.*

He helped her over the rail and noticed she wasn't even breathing hard.

"Are you all right?" she said, giving him the once-over as she straightened her dress. "Where are you bleeding from?"

"What? Oh . . . only a little of that's mine."

He recounted what happened in the grove.

She glanced between him and the dark pool of the ravine. "And you didn't see who it was who saved you?"

"Not a hair, not a trace."

She nodded, looking around. "Typical."

"What's that mean?" And then he realized she didn't look the least bit shocked or worried.

"It means the organization is looking out for you."

"What organization? Those 'friends' you mentioned earlier? Who—?"

She pivoted and held up a hand to shush him. "Hear that?"

He heard a car engine gunning in the ravine. No way that could be his. They both leaned over the rail, squinting into the dark.

"When I was hiding down there I saw another van just like the one that drove us off the road. On my way back up here I noticed that the two guys I gassed were gone."

"You think they've taken the bodies with them?"

"I'll bet on it. This wasn't a couple of beered-up Teamsters. These people had a plan and they were following it by the numbers, military style."

Patrick noticed her stiffen, as if a bell had just rung. "What?"

She shook her head. "Nothing."

As the sound of the van's engine faded, Patrick stared again into the dark ravine, trying to locate his BMW, and was struck by how perfectly their "accident" had been planned. If he had trouble locating his car in the shadows below—and he had a fair idea where it should be—a passing car wouldn't have a clue.

A shudder cut through his body. He began to tremble inside.

"Don't tell me 'nothing,' " he said. "Somebody tried to kill us and—"

"They were going to shoot me up with something first . . . to ask me questions."

"Oh, Christ! What are we into here? Who *were* they?"

"SimGen, I suspect."

"No way! With their clout in court and congress, they don't need to hire killers."

"Who's got more to lose?"

"No, Romy, I don't buy it—I won't buy it. They're—"

She leaned close. Intensity radiated from her like heat from a reactor core. "They're hiding something, Patrick. And whatever it is, the two of us—you, me—we've touched a nerve. We've somehow threatened that secret."

"Just great," he said. "One of the largest corporations in the world has painted a bull's-eye on my back." He held up his hands and watched them shake. "Look at me—I'm a wreck."

Romy held out her own trembling hands. "Just excess adrenaline. It'll pass. The all-important question is: Have they scared you off?"

"Me? Scared off?" he said, hoping he sounded a lot braver than he felt. "Not likely. You see, they made a big mistake when they ruined my practice: it left me with only one client. I *can't* quit."

Romy smiled at him, and he sensed genuine regard in her eyes. Somehow that made the terrors of the past few minutes almost worthwhile. Almost.

"And I'll tell you something else," he said, feeling a growing anger blunt the edge of his fear. "I'm still not convinced SimGen was behind what happened here, but just in case it was, I'm putting them on notice."

Her eyes never left his face. "How?"

"I'm sure I saw the word 'SimGen' on the side of the van that sideswiped us. How about you?"

"Come to think of it," she said, touching an index finger to her temple, "I believe I did too."

"Of course you did. We'll make sure it's in the police report, and I'm going to mention it in every interview over the next week or so. SimGen will deny it of course, but a suspicion will be implanted in the public mind. SimGen will be *praying* nothing happens to us."

"I love it," she said. "Turns the tables in a wonderfully underhanded way."

"I aced Underhanded 101 and 102 in law school."

Just then another set of headlights appeared around the curve. Romy stepped out and waved. This one stopped.

9

Sussex County

"Yessir," Luca Portero said for what seemed like the hundredth or thousandth time, trying to calm the angry voice on the other end of the encrypted line. "I understand, sir."

Truth was, he didn't understand. Not one damn bit.

He rubbed his burning eyes. Somewhere outside this sealed office in the subbasement of SimGen's basic research building, the sun was preparing to rise. Luca hadn't slept in twenty-three hours, but he wasn't the least bit physically tired. The fatigue weighing on him like a lead-lined shroud was mental, from hammering his brain for an explanation as to how such a simple op could go so fatally wrong.

"*Do* you understand, Portero?" said the voice.

It belonged to Darryl Lister, next stop up the food chain from Luca, who was understandably upset about being awakened before his alarm clock with the news that two of his men were dead. He'd hung up on Luca, then called him back half an hour later—after checking with the higher ups, no doubt.

"Then maybe," Lister continued, "just maybe you can help *me* understand how you send out six seasoned pros to process a couple of soft-shelled yuppies, and two come back in body bags, while the yups are still walking around. You were running the op. Explain, please."

Luca reviewed the set-up of the operation, looking for a flaw: he'd hand-picked the men, all seasoned operatives. Using a bogus identity he'd personally rented the vans from two different companies—could have used unmarked SimGen vehicles but didn't want to chance a trace had they needed to abandon one. Then last night, after weeks of surveillance on Sullivan and Cadman, a golden opportunity dropped into his lap: the two of them driving through Westchester in the dead hours of the morning. A couple of quick calls and everyone was in position, waiting for it to go down.

So far, so good. Not a hint that it was going to go down the toilet.

He reran his mental tape of what he'd learned from debriefing the survivors. According to Snyder and Lowery—the wheel man and his back-up in the first van—the hit on Sullivan's car had been perfect: over the rail and down the slope. As planned, they'd driven away and left their rented van at a body shop that knows how to keep a secret.

After that the story murked up. The two survivors, Cruz and Hooper, had spent too much time recovering from their doses of Mace to be of much use. And they were still limping from the tap dance the Cadman woman had done on their balls.

Luca shook his head as rage and admiration did battle within him. Some kind of broad, that Romy. She'd made asses of two of his best men. And maybe they were still alive because of it.

When Cruz and Hooper could finally see and walk again, they'd found Ricker and Green dead; they gathered up the corpses and hauled ass out of there in the second van.

"I put Ricker in charge of the op," Luca said.

"Good choice," Lister replied. "I'd have done the same. But Ricker is dead, and that's what really disturbs me, Portero. How does Ricker wind up with a cracked skull? Who do you know who could take Ricker in hand-to-hand?"

"Nobody."

"Damn right. He was a fucking animal."

No argument there. Ricker wasn't just big and tough and mean, he was experienced, and he was smart. No one was going to take him down without a struggle, and not without him taking one or two of his attackers down with him. But according to Cruz and Hooper, they never heard a sound.

And the condition of Ricker's body . . . his throat had been crushed—that explained the silence—and his head looked like he'd leaned out of a speeding subway and got clocked by a steel support girder. Same with Green.

In fact, if Luca wasn't so sure it was impossible, he'd think someone had grabbed Ricker and Green by their necks and smashed their heads together . . . like a bully brother breaking his sister's dolls. But no one could manhandle two guys as fit and muscular as Ricker and Green that way.

Could they?

An icy length of barbed wire dragged along Luca's spine.

"According to you," Lister said, "Ricker and the team didn't know where they were going until less than an hour before they hit the road. Even you didn't know. So how did whoever took them out know? Sounds to me like they were already there waiting."

"It's more likely the team was followed."

"But why follow them at all? Unless . . . shit! The Japs! I bet it's the Japs! That goddamn Kaze Group has been sticking its dirty fingers deeper and deeper into the biotech pie, and now—"

"I doubt it's the Japs, sir," Luca said. "There's no gain in it. A precedent-setting case would ruin the market for them as well, so they've got no reason to protect Sullivan."

"Maybe they just want to keep our side distracted, off balance."

An unsettling suspicion was taking hold. Luca hesitated to speak it, as if uttering the words aloud might crystallize the possibility into a reality. But he wasn't going to protect Lister from this. Let Lister's gut do a little crawl as well.

"I think there's a new player in the game, sir."

"Have you been drinking? Where'd you get an idea like that?"

"A gut feeling. And the fact that we've never had to deal with a countermove like this."

A pause while Lister digested that. "Who on earth?"

"I have no idea—yet. But I'm going to find out."

"You do that. But don't lose us any more men in the process. Whoever these people are, they play rough."

"Rough," Luca said, clenching his teeth. "They don't know rough. Not by half."

"And something *you* should know," Lister said. "Word from upstairs is they think this was a bad idea."

"Bad?" Anger dueled with a sudden stab of cold fear. "They approved!"

"Be that as it may, they now say the lawyer is not key. If he goes, he can be replaced in minutes by another lawyer, maybe a better one, who'll continue the case and maybe cause even more problems."

"Right," Luca said through his teeth. "No shortage of lawyers."

"The sims—this *particular* group of sims—are key. No other group has come forward looking to unionize, only these. Why, we don't know. Why, we don't care. The point is, the focus of your efforts from this moment on is the Beacon Ridge sims. Are we clear on that?"

"Completely."

Luca already was germinating an idea. A very simple plan. A one-man job. And he knew just the man.

This time there'd be no slip-ups because he'd take care of it himself.

Because, in a way, this had become personal.

Romy Cadman had made him look bad. Hurt his reputation. Now she was going to hurt.

10

Westchester

"Now I understand why you insisted I take all that martial arts training," Romy said.

She stood in an empty lady's room speaking to Zero on the secure cell phone he'd given her. It was clear after last night that she was under surveillance, so she'd picked a spot at random and wound up in a coffee shop not far from the federal district courthouse in White Plains. At this hour—10:32 A.M.—the dining area contained only a handful of late breakfasters; it was too early for lunch, so the ladies room was empty; she'd checked all the stalls before calling.

"To be honest, I always thought the possibility of your ever being in physical danger remote, but I felt it best you be prepared for it."

"If nothing else, it helped me keep my cool."

Relative cool, she thought. Her nerves were still jangled. She'd tried to catch some sleep at the motel—in her own room, much to Patrick's dismay—but it had remained steadfastly out of reach; so she'd compensated this morning by drinking too much coffee, which did nothing to settle her nerves.

She caught sight of herself in one of the mirrors. A little haggard looking, maybe, but not half bad for someone who'd ducked an attempt on her life just a few hours ago.

"But murder?" she said. "Somehow I don't see the brothers Sinclair sitting around and deciding to have us killed."

"I doubt they did. That decision was reached elsewhere, I'm sure. By someone connected to the company but with his own best interests at heart."

"Someone also connected to Manassas Ventures, perhaps?"

"Perhaps. Our ongoing investigation into that mysterious little company keeps coming up empty. It seems to exist in a vacuum. We've avoided direct inquiries, keeping everything back door because we don't want to let them know anyone's interested. But if nothing pans out soon we may have to arrange a little accident."

"Accident?"

He ignored her. "In the meantime we want to keep you and Patrick alive and well. Connecting SimGen to the vans was a brilliant stroke. Your idea?"

"No. Patrick's."

"Clever fellow. The Beacon Ridge sims could do a lot worse."

"I'm beginning to see that." After last night, despite his tough talk, she'd half expected him to wake up this morning and run off with his tail tucked between his legs.

But he was in court now, arguing motions. "What I don't see is how you managed to be down in that ravine with us."

"*I* wasn't there."

"I don't mean you personally—the organization."

"We had a tail on Portero."

That startled her. "For how long?"

"Long enough to see him rent a couple of vans. After that, we kept an eye on the vans. When some mercenary types became attached to the vans, I knew some strong-arm tactics were in the works. Some of our people followed one van to that ravine and intervened when they saw no alternative."

"I'm glad they did."

"The gloves are off, I'm afraid. The organization is going to mount its own surveillance on you and Patrick. The Beacon Ridge barrack as well."

Romy's stomach turned. "Oh, no. You don't think—"

"Anything is possible. And we must be prepared for it."

11

Westchester County

"I've got to tell you," Patrick said to Romy as they sat in the sim barrack, "after what I saw last week, I'm not as comfortable with this as I used to be."

Anj was going through her now standard routine of draping herself across Patrick's lap whenever he visited. He'd found it cute before; a warm-fuzzy moment. But now . . .

"That's understandable," she said. "You never viewed them in a sexual context before."

"I still don't . . . can't." The memory of the brothel still gave his gut a squeamish twist. "But knowing that other people do . . ."

She was out from the city again, checking on her investment, as she liked to put it. For the past week Patrick had entertained a faint hope that their ordeal in the ravine might forge a bond that would lead to a closer, more intimate relationship. That hope was fading. Romy remained all business.

"You haven't been scared off then?" she said.

"I'm not looking to be a martyr, but no."

She smiled. "I never took you for the martyr type."

"You mean there's a martyr type? Who the hell would want to be a martyr?"

"More than you'd think. In the right setting it can be a form of celebrity."

"I guess so. Who was it who said that some people climb onto the cross merely to be seen from a greater distance?"

"Camus, I believe."

"Right." Patrick was startled—happily. "You've read Camus?"

She shrugged.

Here was a side of Romy that Patrick had never imagined. He wanted to delve deeper but she steered him right back to business.

"Do you see any legal speed bumps ahead?" she asked.

"Not in the immediate future," he began, then noticed Tome hovering at his shoulder.

"'Scuse, Mist Sulliman, but Anj must eat." He tugged the sleeve of the young sim's T-shirt. "Come, Anj. Dinner come." As he led her toward the tables, Tome turned and said, "You eat too?"

Patrick glanced around. Most of the sims had gone through the line and were chowing down. He eyed the rich dark stew being ladled from the big pot and wasn't even tempted.

"No, thanks, Tome. I'm, uh, cutting back."

Romy lowered her voice. "Maybe we should give it a try. Just a taste . . . to be good guests."

"It's made from dining room leftovers," he whispered from a corner of his mouth.

"I believe I'll pass too," Romy called out, then turned to Patrick. "By the way, are you still living in that motel?"

"Still."

"Aren't you cramped?"

"Yes and no. I thought I'd go nuts in a place like that—you know, without all my things. But I've found I don't miss them as much as I thought I would. No house, no furniture, no office, no status car . . . I should be in a deep depression but oddly enough I'm not. I've got this strange, light feeling . . . unencumbered, I guess you could say. I feel as if I've been cut free from weights I didn't even know were there. That sound weird to you?"

"No," she said softly, and he thought he detected some warmth in her smile. "Not weird at all." She seemed to catch herself and looked away in the direction of the sims. "By the way, if we're not eating here, where do you suggest?"

"How do you feel about Cajun food?"

"Love it. I'll eat anything blackened—catfish, redfish, potholders, you name it."

"Great. I know this little place in Mount Kisco . . ."

They talked about their favorite foods—one of Romy's was sushi which, despite heroic efforts, Patrick had never developed a taste for. He was beginning to believe that the evening was shaping up to be ripe with promise when a loud groan and a clatter interrupted them.

Patrick turned and saw that one of the caddie sims had knocked his plate off the table and was doubled over, clutching his abdomen. As he watched, a second sim slipped off the bench and slumped to her knees, groaning.

"What the hell's going on?" Patrick said.

But Romy was already on her feet. "Oh, God!" she cried. "Something's wrong with the food!" She rushed forward, shouting. "Don't eat the food! It's bad! *Bad!*"

Too late. Patrick watched helplessly as one sim after another doubled over and crumpled to the floor, writhing in pain.

"What is it?" he said. "Ptomaine?"

She shook her head, her face ashen. "Spoiled food doesn't act this quickly. They've been poisoned, damn it! Somebody's poisoned their food!"

Patrick pulled out his cell phone and punched in 911. "I'll call an ambulance—*lots* of ambulances!"

"To take them where?"

"To the emer—" He stopped. "Shit!"

"Right. No hospital's going to take them. They're not human."

"Then how about a veterinary hospital?"

"Is there one around? And even if there is, how do we get them there? I don't know of an ambulance service in the world that'll transport animals." She pulled out her own phone. "But I know someone . . ."

"This organization of yours?"

She glanced at him, then turned away, rapidly punching buttons, then speaking softly into her phone.

Patrick had to do something. With frustration mounting to the detonation point he looked around and saw Tome still standing.

"Tome! You didn't eat?"

The older sim shook his head. "Not chance."

"Get up to the clubhouse! Fast! Tell them you've all been poisoned!"

As Tome ran off, Patrick hurried to the dorm area and began pulling blankets and pillows from the bunks. He couldn't do anything about whatever toxin had been used to poison them, but at least he could try to make the sims more comfortable.

"Good idea," Romy said, close by. He looked up and saw her beside him with an armful of blankets. "Help is on the way."

"Who? How much?"

"I don't know."

They hurried back to the eating area where it looked like a bomb had exploded: benches on their sides, tipped tables, spilled trays, and moaning, pain-wracked casualties strewn about the floor. Patrick recognized Nabb, his caddie when he'd played golf here—the last time he'd *ever* play golf here—that fateful September day he became involved with these sims. He lay doubled over on his side, arms folded across his abdomen.

"Here you go, buddy," he said, slipping a pillow under his head.

"Hurt, Mist Sulliman," Nabb groaned. "Hurt ver bad."

He draped a blanket over him. "I know, Nabb. We're getting help."

He spotted Deek, another caddie he knew, and tried to make him comfortable. He noticed the big sim's bruised face and remembered being told how clumsy he was.

"Why hurt, Mist Sulliman?" Deek said, looking up at him with watery brown eyes. "Why?"

89

"Because someone . . ." A blast of fury forced him to stop and look away. Who? Who would or could do something like this? He found it incomprehensible.

"Sweet Jesus!" someone gasped.

Patrick looked up and saw Holmes Carter and a slim, dapper man he didn't recognize standing behind Tome in the barrack doorway. The stranger moved into the room, leaving the pudgy Carter alone, looking like a possum frozen in the glare of oncoming headlights.

"Tome wasn't kidding!" the stranger said to no one in particular. "What happened here?"

"They started getting sick after eating the stew," Patrick said. "Who are you?"

"Dr. Stokes. I'm an anesthesiologist. And I already know who you are." He didn't offer to shake hands; instead he knelt beside one of the sick sims, a female. "This one doesn't look so hot."

Tell me something I don't already know, Patrick wanted to say, but bit his tongue.

"None of them do. Can you help?"

"I'm not a vet."

Romy's eyes implored him. "Help them! Please! You treat humans. How much closer to human can you get?"

Dr. Stokes nodded. "Point taken. Let's see what I can do."

As he began pressing on the sim's abdomen, asking her questions, Patrick glanced around and spotted a small, huddled form under one of the tables. With a cold band tightening around his chest, he rushed over—Anj. She lay curled into a tight, shuddering ball.

"Anj?" Patrick crouched beside her and touched her shoulder; her T-shirt was soaked. "Anj, speak to me."

A whimper was her only reply. Patrick gathered her into his arms—Christ, she was wringing wet—and carried her over to Dr. Stokes. Her face was so pale.

"This one's just a baby," he told Stokes. "And she's real bad."

Patrick gently lay Anj on the floor between them. Romy was there immediately with a pillow and blanket.

"Diaphoretic," Stokes said, more to himself than Patrick. He held her wrist a moment. "Pulse is thready."

"What's that mean?"

"She's going into shock." He turned back to the first sim he'd been examining. "This one too. They're going to need IVs and pressors. What in God's name did they eat?"

Before Patrick could answer, he heard the sound of a heavy-duty engine, slamming doors, and Carter saying, "You can't drive that up here!"

He looked up and saw two grim-faced men, one in a golf shirt, the other in a sport coat, file through the door with some kind of cart rolling between them. They pushed past Carter as if he were a piece of misplaced furniture. Two more strangers, a man and a woman, both in flannel shirts and jeans, followed them.

"You can't just walk in here!" Carter said. "This is a private club!"

Ignoring him, they pulled stethoscopes and blood pressure cuffs from the cart and fanned out into the room. The woman came over to where Patrick, Romy, and Stokes stood. She looked to be in her forties, her long brown hair streaked with gray and tied back. Without a word she knelt beside Anj and the other sim and began taking blood pressures.

"They're shocky," Stokes offered.

The woman looked up. Her face was expressionless, all business, but her eyes looked infinitely sad. "You a doc?"

"Yes, I'm an—"

"We've got saline in the cart. If you want to help, you can start drips on these two."

Stokes nodded and headed for the cart. The stranger moved on.

Patrick turned to Romy. "Who are these people?"

"Doctors."

"From SimGen?"

She shook her head and bit her upper lip. Romy's usually steely composure had slipped. She looked rattled, something Patrick never would have thought possible. Maybe it was the helplessness. Patrick felt it too—a need to do something but not knowing what.

"Your people then," he said. "Your organization. How'd they get here so fast?"

"They've been on standby."

"You mean you expected this?"

"Expected someone might try to hurt them." Her eyes were black cauldrons. "Excuse me. I need a little air."

He watched her breeze past Holmes Carter, still standing by the door, sputtering like an over-choked engine. Tome squatted against a far wall, his face buried in his arms. And all around Patrick, the strange, silent doctors, gliding from one sick sim to another.

Feeling useless, he decided he could use a breath of night air himself, but first he had something to say . . .

He stopped before Carter. "This your doing, Holmesy?"

Carter's round face reddened, his third chin wobbled. "You son of a bitch! If I was going to poison anyone it would be you, not these dumb animals. They're just pawns in your game."

The genuine outrage in Carter's eyes made Patrick regret his words. He backed off a bit. "Well . . . somebody poisoned them."

"If you're looking to place blame, Sullivan, find a mirror. This never would have happened if you hadn't started poking your nose where it doesn't belong."

Stung, Patrick turned away. The heartbreaking truth of Carter's words clung to his shoulders as he stepped out into the night.

Some sort of oversized commuter van was parked on the grass outside. The doctors had driven it straight across the club's rear lawn to the barrack door; Patrick could trace the deep furrows under the pitiless glow of the moon peering down from the crystal sky. Up on the rise he spotted a number of Beacon Ridge members standing outside the clubhouse, gawking at the scene. And Romy . . . where was Romy?

He walked around the barrack and spotted her down the slope by the border privet hedge. But she wasn't alone. A tall dark figure stood beside her. After a moment, Romy turned and began walking back up the slope; the tall man faded into the shadows of the hedge.

"Who was that?" he asked as she approached.

"No one."

"But—"

Her face had settled into grim lines. "You didn't see a thing. Now let's go back inside and make ourselves useful."

Patrick was about to comment on what seemed to be a lot of hush-hush, undercover nonsense but bit it back when he realized it wasn't nonsense at all. Not when poison was part of someone's game plan.

Romy stopped dead in the doorway and he ran into her back, knocking her forward. He saw immediately why she'd stopped.

Chaos in the barrack. The formerly silent, seemingly imperturbable doctors were in frenzied motion, pumping ventilation bags and thumping sim chests.

"I've got another one crashing here!" one called out. He was on his knees next to a supine sim. He looked up and saw Romy and Patrick. "You two want to help?"

Patrick tried to speak but could only nod.

"Name it," Romy said.

"Each of you get an Ambu bag from that cart and bring them over here."

Romy was already moving. "What's an Am—?"

"Looks like a small football with a face mask attached," the doctor said.

Romy opened a deep drawer, removed two of the devices, handed one to Patrick. On their way back, to his right, he noticed Holmes Carter kneeling, pumping air into a sim's lungs.

Carter . . . ?

To his left, the woman doc waved and called out. "You—with the Ambu! Over here! Quick!"

Romy peeled off and Patrick kept on course toward the first doc. He stuttered to a stop when he saw the patient.

Anj.

She lay supine on the floor, limp as a rag doll with half its stuffing gone; the front of her bib overalls had been pulled down and her T-shirt slit open, exposing her budding, pink-nippled, lightly furred but otherwise very human-looking breasts.

"Don't just stand there!" the doctor said. He was sweaty, flushed, and looked too young to be a doctor. He had his hands between Anj's breasts and was pumping on her chest. "Bag her!"

Patrick's frozen brain tried to make sense of the words as they filtered through air thick as cotton.

"Bag . . . ?" Was she dead?

"Give me that!" The doctor reached across Anj and snatched the Ambu bag from Patrick's numb fingers. He fitted the mask over Anj's mouth and nose and squeezed the bag. "There! Do that once for every five times I pump."

Patrick dropped to his knees and managed to get his hands to work, squeezing the bag every time the doctor shouted "Now!" and wishing someone would cover her. Every so often the doctor would stop pumping and press his stethoscope to Anj's chest.

"Shit!" he said after the third time. "Nothing! Keep bagging." He pawed through what looked like an orange plastic tool box, muttering, "No monitor, no defibrillator, how am I supposed to . . . here!"

95

He pulled out a small syringe capped with a three- or four-inch needle. He popped the top, expelled air and a little fluid, then swabbed Anj's chest with alcohol.

Patrick blinked. "You're not going to stick that into—"

That was exactly what he did: right between a pair of ribs to the left of her breast bone; he drew back on the plunger until a gush of dark red swirled into the barrel, then emptied the syringe.

The doctor resumed pumping, crying, "One-two-three-four-five-*bag*!"

They kept up the routine for another minute or so, then the doctor listened to Anj's chest again.

"Nothing." He pulled a penlight from the plastic box and flashed it into her eyes. "Fixed and dilated." He leaned back and wiped his dripping face on his sleeve. "She's gone."

"No," Patrick said.

But Anj's glazed, staring eyes said it all. Still he began squeezing the bag again, frantically, spasmodically.

"No use," the doctor said.

"Try, damn it!" Patrick shouted. "She's too young! She's too . . . " He ran out of words.

"Her brain's been deprived of oxygen too long. She's not coming back."

Patrick dropped the bag and leaned over her. An aching pressure built in his chest. He began to cry, huge sobs tearing free from deep within.

A hand closed gently on his shoulder and he heard the young doctor say, "I know how you feel."

Patrick shrugged off his hand. "No, you don't."

"I do, believe me. We couldn't save her, but we've got other sick sims here and maybe we can save some of *them*. Let's get to work."

"All right," Patrick said, unable to buck the doctor's logic. "Just give me a minute."

As the doctor moved off, Patrick pulled the edges of Anj's torn T-shirt together. They didn't quite meet so he pulled up the bib front of her overalls. Then he pushed her eyelids closed and stared at her.

How could he feel such a sense of loss for someone, something that wasn't even human? This wasn't like puddling up at the end of "Old Yeller." This was *real*.

He pulled off his suit coat and draped it over the upper half of her body. He hovered by her side a moment longer; then, feeling like a terminally arthritic hundred-year-old man, he pushed himself to his feet and moved on.

The next half hour became a staggering blur, moving from one prostrate form to another, losing sim after sim, and pressing on, until . . . finally . . . it was over.

Spent, Patrick leaned against a wall, counting. He felt as if he'd been dragged behind a truck over forty miles of bad road. He'd cried tonight. When was the last time he'd cried? Romy sagged against him, still sobbing. He counted twice, three times, but the number kept coming up the same: nineteen still, sheet-covered forms strewn about the floor.

The woman doctor they'd met earlier drifted by; he flagged her down.

"How many did you save?" he said.

She brushed a damp ringlet away from her flushed face. "Six—just barely. We've moved them into the sleep area. They'll make it, but it'll be weeks before they're back to normal. Counting the older sim who didn't eat, that leaves seven survivors."

"The bastards!" Romy gritted through her teeth. "The lousy fucking bastards!"

She pushed away from him and strode for the door, pounding the wall with her fist.

Patrick felt too physically and emotionally drained to go after her. He saw Tome crouched in a corner, his head cradled in his arms. Patrick went over and squatted next to him.

"I'm sorry, Tome," he said, feeling the words catch in his throat. "I'm so sorry."

Tome looked up at him with reddened eyes; tears streaked his cheeks. "Sim family gone, Mist Sulliman. All gone."

"Not all, Tome. Deek survived, so did some others."

But Tome was shaking his head. "Too many dead sim. Family gone. All Tome fault."

"No-no-no," Patrick said, putting a hand on his shoulder. "You can't lay that on yourself. If anybody's to blame here—besides the son of a bitch who poisoned the food—it's me."

Tome kept shaking his head. "No. Tome know. Tome ask Mist Sulliman. If Tome nev ask, Mist Sulliman nev do."

"That doesn't make you responsible for . . . this. You wanted something better for your family, Tome, and we're not going to let this stop us. I swear—"

"No, Mist Sulliman. We stop. Family gone. No law bring back. We stop. Other sim die if no stop."

"You can't mean that!" Patrick said, stunned. "That'll mean that Anj and Nabb and all the others died for nothing!"

Tome turned and slid away. "No union, Mist Sulliman. Tome too tired. Tome too sad."

"Then they win! Is that what you want?"

"Tome want sim live," he said without looking back. "That all Tome want now."

Patrick fought the urge to grab the old sim and shake some sense into him. They couldn't quit now—public opinion would rush to their side after this atrocity. He took a step after him, but the utter defeat in the slump of those narrow retreating shoulders stopped him.

He remembered the night they met, when Tome explained what he and the other sims wanted: *Family. . . and one thing other . . . respect, Mist Sulliman. Just little respect.*

And now your family's been murdered, Patrick thought. And the only respect you've gained is mine. And what's that worth?

Flickering light to his left caught his eye. He saw Reverend Eckert's face on the TV screen in the corner. The voice was muted but Patrick knew the bastard could only be spewing more of his anti-sim venom. With a low cry of rage he stalked across the room, picked up an overturned bench, and raised it above his head. But before he could smash the set, a hand grabbed his arm.

"Please don't do that," said a voice.

He turned and found Holmes Carter standing behind him. On any other day he would have teed off on the man, but Carter had surprised the hell out of him tonight—worked as hard as anyone to save the sims. And he looked it: his sport coat was gone and his wrinkled shirt lay partially unbuttoned, exposing a swath of his bulging belly. Right now he looked shell-shocked.

Patrick knew exactly how he felt.

"Why the hell not?"

"What will the survivors watch?"

Damn him, he was right.

Patrick lowered the bench and extended his hand. "I want to thank you, Holmes. I take back anything I've ever said to offend you."

"Sure." Carter gave his hand a listless, distracted shake and looked around. "Gone," he said dazedly. "Just like that, three-quarters of our sims . . . gone. Nabb . . . he used to be my favorite caddie, and now he's dead. Why?" He looked at Patrick with tear-filled eyes. "What kind of sick person would do this? What kind of a world have we created?"

"Wish I knew, Holmes. It gets stranger and stranger."

Carter sighed. "I realized something tonight. These sims . . . they're. . . they were . . . part of Beacon Ridge. We knew them. We liked them. I'm going to tell the board to grant collective bargaining rights, and I'm going to insist that the survivors remain together as long as they want."

Patrick opened his mouth to speak but found himself, for possibly the first time in his adult life, at a loss for words.

Carter smiled wanly. "What's the matter? Cat got your tongue?" He gave his head a single sad shake. "Wasn't that part of the exchange that set this whole mess in motion?"

Patrick nodded, remembering their little confrontation in the club men's room. "Yes . . . yes, I believe it was. This is good of you, Holmes."

"I just wish I'd done it yesterday."

Without another word Carter turned and wove his way through the dead sims toward the door.

We've won, Patrick thought—a reflex. The thought died aborning. He looked around at the sheeted forms and knew that if this was winning, he'd much rather have lost.

He heard an engine rumble to life outside. He looked around and realized that the mysterious doctors had disappeared. He hurried to the door in time to see the truck roll away across the grass toward the road.

Romy stood there, watching. She turned to him and seemed to have regained her composure. He filled her in on the latest developments.

"Tome's decision doesn't surprise me," she said. "Sims aren't fighters. But after what you'd told me about the club president . . ."

"Yeah. I guess I had Holmes wrong. People never cease to surprise me, for good or for ill. Like these phantom doctors of yours. Where did they come from, where did they go? They pop out of nowhere with no explanation, and then they're gone."

"I told you—" Romy began.

"I don't want to hear about some nameless 'organization' again. How about some specifics? Who's behind you? And who killed those two guys when we were run off the road the other night? I want answers, Romy."

Her smile was tight. "Do you? Well then maybe you're in for one more surprise tonight."

"I don't think I can handle another." He noticed a strange look in her eyes, wary yet flirting with anticipation. "But I'll bite. What?"

"Someone wants to meet you."

12

Romy drove them to a small cabin on the edge of Rye Lake. Patrick stepped from her rented car and looked around.

The surrounding woods lay dark and silent; the cabin was an angular blotch of shadow with no sign of habitation; on its far side a dock jutted into the lake where tendrils of mist rose from the glassy moonlit water into the chill air.

"Doesn't look like anyone's home," he said.

Romy was moving toward the cabin. "Look again. And use your nose."

Patrick sniffed the air. A wood fire going somewhere. And now he saw a thin stream of smoke drifting from the cabin's chimney. Okay, so someone was inside. But who? Romy had been tight-lipped during the entire trip, telling him only that he'd find out when they got there. Well, they were here now, and he wanted to know.

Romy was already half way to the door. He caught up with her.

"This cloak-and-dagger stuff is getting to me," he told her.

"Relax. There may be a cloak involved, but no dagger." Without warning she leaned forward and kissed him—too briefly—on the lips. "Thanks."

"What for?"

"For hanging in there tonight. For caring."

She opened the door and pushed through. Patrick touched his mouth where the warmth of Romy's lips lingered, then followed her into the dark interior, lit only by the glow from the fireplace.

"Over here, Romy," said a deep voice near the fire. Patrick could make out a dark form seated in a high-backed chair, positioned so that the light came from behind him. Patrick saw the figure lean forward and extend a hand. "Welcome, Mr. Sullivan."

Hesitantly Patrick stepped forward and shook the hand, surprised to find it was gloved. "And you are . . .?"

"I'm called Zero."

And that stands for what? Patrick thought. IQ? Personality rating? But he said, "Interesting name."

"Forgive the melodramatic trappings," Zero said, "but we take security very seriously."

" 'We?' "

"A loose-knit organization I've put together. Our goal, in a nutshell, is to protect existing sims from exploitation and stop SimGen and anyone else from producing more."

"Tall order."

"We know."

"How many members?"

"Many."

"Like those doctors who showed up tonight?"

"Yes. Volunteers. They were on standby in case disaster struck."

"Which it did—in spades."

"Yes. Mistakenly I expected a more direct form of violence, a bomb or the like. I had the barrack under guard." Zero's voice thickened. "I never thought to guard the kitchen."

Romy said, "So it was one of the help?" The flickering firelight accentuated her high cheekbones, glittered in her eyes.

"I doubt it. That sample of stew you brought me was laced with a very sophisticated synthetic toxin we've been unable to identify. This was not the work of a jealous kitchen hand or a union goon. Whoever did this has considerable resources behind him."

"SimGen," Patrick said.

"Not impossible, but certainly out of character. SimGen has always protected its sims."

"But have its sims ever posed a threat before?"

Romy spoke, nodding. "That's a point, but we're coming to believe that SimGen is not quite the free-standing entity it presents to the public. That it's not pulling all its own strings. This may be the work of another shadow organization within SimGen or linked to it."

"But why kill the Beacon Ridge sims?"

"Because what threatens SimGen," Zero said, "threatens the shadow group. And in this case, the sims were the logical target: lawyers are replaceable, plaintiffs are not."

"Any idea who they are?"

"No, but we've got the start of a trail, and we're following it. That's why I've asked you here tonight, Mr. Sullivan. We'd like your help."

"You want to hire me?"

"Not exactly. You'd be an unpaid consultant, a volunteer like Ms. Cadman."

"I don't work for free."

"Even for the people who saved your life?" Romy said.

She had him there. "Glad you brought that up: just who *did* save my life?"

Zero said, "Join us and you'll know . . . eventually."

"You need me in the legal field?"

"There, and wherever else your unique brand of ingenuity can be of service."

"Flattery will get you everywhere."

"And who knows?" Zero said. "We may be able to position you for another crack at SimGen's deep pockets."

"Now you're talking."

"I knew that would sell you." The pearly enamel within her smile caught the light, giving her a Cheshire Cat look.

"I'm not sold yet. You've been calling the shots for Romy, I assume."

Zero inclined his head. "I merely suggest . . . she is always free to decline, just as you will be."

"But who's calling the shots for you?"

"No one."

"You could be just telling me that."

"I could. But I'm not."

"So you're funding this operation?"

He shook his head. "I raise money in various ways . . . donations from a number of sources."

"I must have missed the last annual *Free the Sims* Telethon."

No one laughed. Tough crowd, Patrick thought.

"Your point?" Zero said.

"Money tends to come with strings."

"True. And these donations come with one string, and only one: Stop SimGen."

"What about freeing the sims?"

"That will be the fallout, but first we shut down the pipeline. Once we cut off the flow of new sims, we can deal with the problem of what to do with those who already exist."

"These donors . . . who are they—specifically? I like to know who's footing the bill."

"I will partially answer that when you join us, with the proviso that you never breathe a word of what you learn. But I must warn you not to accept my invitation lightly. The deeper you delve into this morass, the more you'll see that nothing connected with it is what it appears to be. And there's danger. You've witnessed firsthand on more than one occasion the ruthlessness of the other side. We're in a war, Mr. Sullivan, and any one of us could become a casualty."

Patrick swallowed. Where had his saliva gone? But if Romy was in this and willing to take the risks, how could he stand here next to her and back out? What kind of a man would that make him?

Perhaps a man who'd live to a ripe old age.

But he managed a shrug that conveyed a lot more bravado that he felt. "Okay, I'm in. Do I have to sign in blood or anything like that?"

Zero laughed—a strangely high-pitched sound. "Excellent!" He raised his hand and a TV flickered to life on the far side of the room. Diagonal lines danced across the screen, then the Reverend Eckert's face appeared.

"Jerk!" Patrick said.

"Give him a listen."

Eckert's face looked grave, anguished. His voice was at least an octave lower than his usual ranting tone.

"My friends . . . I have just heard that a number of sims—nineteen of them, I'm told—have been killed. Poisoned. These were the sims who were trying to unionize. This is very disturbing. More than disturbing, it's a terrible, terrible thing, and I hope, I pray to the Good Lord that no one in my flock is responsible. Because if one of you is, then I must shoulder some of the blame as well, because it might have been my words that drove one of you to this terrible deed. If that is the case, then I have been misunderstood. Terribly misunderstood.

"So hear me now, friends, and hear me well.

"I wish no harm to any sim. I have never, ever preached violence against them. I have said they were created by evil, Satan-inspired science, and I know that to be true, but I have never said the sims themselves were evil. They are not. They are the innocent products of unnatural science who should be allowed to live out their lives in peace.

"Violence toward sims is not the way. If you kill sims, you only give SinGen the excuse to produce more. We want SinGen to stop producing sims. We must use the

law—the law, *my friends—to cut off the supply of sims at its source by piercing the beating evil heart of the problem. And that heart is the devil corporation that subverts the Laws of Creation by creating creatures that are not part of God's design.*

"Please. I beg of you: Do not harm sims. That is not the answer—it is, in fact, counterproductive. Spreading the word, boycotting businesses that lease sims, endlessly harassing SinGen in court until it finally surrenders. That is the way, my friends. The only way.

"And to continue fighting that battle, I need your support . . ."

The screen went blank.

"His standard request for contributions follows," Zero said.

"When did he broadcast that?" Patrick said.

"He hasn't. He rushed it into production and it's going out to replace his previously scheduled message."

"How'd you get it?"

"The Reverend Eckert is part of the organization. One of its major contributors, in fact."

For the second time tonight Patrick found himself speechless.

Romy laughed. "If only you could see your face! Oh, God, I wish I had a camera!"

13

Sussex County

As soon as Luca stepped into the room, the usually listless Sinclair-2 rose from his seat and came toward him. He looked like he'd slept in his clothes; his face flushed as he started shouting.

"It was you, wasn't it? You monster! You *monster*!"

"Calm down, Ellis," Able Voss said, putting an arm around the man's shoulders. "You can't go makin wild accusations like that."

"I can!" Sinclair-2 cried. "I know this man's methods. And if he didn't do it himself, he sent one of his hired thugs!"

No, Luca thought. I did it myself. A one-man op. That's what you have to do sometimes if you want to be sure a job gets done right.

It had taken Luca about a week after the Saw Mill River Parkway debacle to put all the pieces in place. Two nights ago he'd made his move.

But the op developed an early hitch: a tail. If he hadn't been looking for one, he never would have spotted it. But he'd been prepared.

He'd driven into midtown Manhattan and valet-parked his car at the New Yorker Hotel, then hurried through the lobby and out a side exit where he hailed a cab that took him to a second car that had been left for him in a lot in the theater district. He'd driven out of town immediately, directly to Westchester where he'd parked a good mile from the Beacon Ridge Country Club. He'd walked the rest of the way, ducking into the shadows whenever a car approached. When he reached the club, he'd huddled in the hedges until the sims were all in their barrack and the last human had left.

Or so he'd thought. That was when he'd almost got caught. He'd been just about to step out of the bushes when he spotted two dark figures gliding between the shadows near the barrack. As he'd watched they separated, one swiftly climbing a tree, the other disappearing into the bushes.

Someone had the sim quarters under guard. Sullivan? Cadman? No matter. That hadn't been Luca's destination. He was headed for the sprawling structure on the crest of the hill, the club's main building.

Soon he'd reached his destination: the kitchen. Once he'd located the cooking pot labeled "*SIMS*" he removed a vial of clear odorless liquid from his breast pocket. A brand new compound, so new it didn't have a name yet, only a number: J7683452.

He'd emptied the vial into the big pot and begun swirling the liquid around, coating the sides and bottom. When it dried, it was invisible. The only thing that could

have gone wrong was somebody washing out the pot. But it had been hung up clean, so that was unlikely.

Amazing stuff, J7683452. He could have stuck his head into that pot, licked its insides clean, and he'd be fine. Perfectly harmless in that state. But heat it to a hundred-and-sixty degrees or more and . . .

Bon appétit.

As for here and now, he didn't owe the Sinclair brothers an explanation. And they didn't deserve one.

Keeping his expression bland, his voice low, Luca said, "Just what do you think I or one of my so-called thugs have supposedly done?"

"Don't play games, Portero! The Beacon Ridge sims —nineteen of them murdered last night!"

"Murdered?" he said with a calculatedly derisive snort—few things gave him more pleasure than getting under these twits' skins. "They're animals. They can be killed, they can be slaughtered, they can be sacrificed to the gods, but they can't be murdered."

With a roar like a bull ape, Sinclair-2 launched himself at Luca, only to be hauled back by the heavier, stronger Voss.

"You don't want to be doin that, son," Voss said. "Trust me, you don't."

"Ellis, for God's sake control yourself!" Sinclair-1 said.

"Listen to them," Luca said softly.

He hadn't moved a muscle. He'd take no pleasure in hurting Sinclair-2—it would be like fighting a woman—but he could not allow another man to lay a hand on him without some form of retaliation.

Sinclair-2 struggled a moment, then pulled free and returned to his usual spot on the sofa where he dropped his face into his hands and sobbed.

What gives with that guy? Luca wondered. How can he be such a wimp?

"Did you?" Sinclair-1 said, staring at him. "Were you responsible for poisoning those sims?"

"Does it matter?" Luca said.

No one answered.

Just as I thought. They don't *want* to know.

"Just tell me one thing," Voss said. "And think very carefully on your answer: Will the perpetrator or perpetrators ever be found?"

"My guess?" Luca shook his head. "Never. But whoever they were, they did us a favor. The Beacon Ridge club has surrendered. They're giving the sims what they want."

"Since when?" Voss said. "I ain't heard nothin about this."

"That's because they haven't made the announcement yet."

"If that's true," the attorney said, his eyes widening, "it takes the matter out of the court's hands."

"No precedent," Sinclair-1 whispered.

Luca watched cautious optimism grow in their eyes. He'd be sharing in that if not for a rumor that had filtered back to him this morning. Nothing more than a rumor, he hoped—*prayed*. Nothing more than a wild fantasy cooked up by some drugged-out waste of protoplasm. He'd keep it to himself for now. Lister suspected a leak somewhere, and if he was right, the less said, the better.

But he dearly wished he could lay it on these two. The mere mention now of what he'd heard would snuff out the relief warming Sinclair-1 and Voss as if it had never been.

Because if the rumor was even half true, it would make the threat they'd just overcome seem like a pebble in a mountain gorge.